PRAISE FOR *KRAKOW MELT*:

"Strange, provocative, and daring: al̶̶̶̶̶̶̶̶̶̶̶̶̶̶̶̶̶̶̶ ̶̶̶̶̶̶̶̶̶̶̶̶̶ ̶̶̶̶̶̶ ̶̶ ̶̶̶̶̶̶̶̶̶̶ ̶̶̶̶̶̶ Daniel Allen Cox's work. In *Krakow Melt*, the writer gets stranger, more provocative, and more daring. Best of all, he's given us a novel that's both thrilling and fun to read."
—Scott Heim, author of *Mysterious Skin* and *We Disappear*

"I've been a fan of Daniel Allen Cox's writing for some time, and in *Krakow Melt* the wit, punch, and sexual heat of *Shuck* return, revved up even more. As we read, we slip into a free zone of writing, almost as if the boundaries of the page had themselves slipped away and we were free to wander through Eastern Europe like natives, with the haunted and nomadic gaze of those on whom history has given up. Cox brings us a story of struggle, defeat, liberation, and love that I will never forget."
—Kevin Killian, author of *Spreadeagle* and *Impossible Princess*

"*Krakow Melt* is Syd Barrett crossed with the Polish queer nation, a rollicking and heart-pounding urban jump through some grim realities and fine prose stylings."
—Zoe Whittall, author of *Bottle Rocket Hearts* and *Holding Still For As Long As Possible*

KRAKOW MELT

Daniel Allen Cox

ARSENAL PULP PRESS | VANCOUVER

KRAKOW MELT
Copyright © 2010 by Daniel Allen Cox

ARSENAL PULP PRESS
#101-211 East Georgia St.
Vancouver, BC
Canada V6A 1Z6
arsenalpulp.com

The publisher gratefully acknowledges the support of the Canada Council for
the Arts and the British Columbia Arts Council for its publishing program, and
the Government of Canada through the Book Publishing Industry Development
Program and the Government of British Columbia through the Book Publishing
Tax Credit Program for its publishing activities.

This is a work of fiction. Any resemblance of characters to persons either living
or deceased is purely coincidental.

Editing by Susan Safyan
Cover design by Farah Khan, *house9design.ca*
Author photograph by Dallas Curow, *dallascurow.com*

Printed and bound in Canada on 100% post-consumer recycled paper

Library and Archives Canada Cataloguing in Publication

Cox, Daniel Allen
          Krakow melt / Daniel Allen Cox.

Also available in electronic format.
ISBN 978-1-55152-372-9

          I. Title.

PS8605.O934K73 2010   C813'.6   C2010-903339-6

For Mark

and for those who can still smell the fire

NOWA HUTA

Kraków is crows. Big, floppy ones. I don't live in the city centre but in Nowa Huta, a suburb a few kilometres east. We can still hear them squawking from so far away, yammering on about the histories. I do a bit of that myself.

Nowa Huta was originally designed without a church. I love it for other reasons, too.

The Central Square explodes into a grid of side streets and tributaries lined with giant cement apartment blocks. It looks better than it sounds; this is the best of Soviet and Renaissance design, melded together. There used to be a statue of Vladimir Lenin in the Plac Centralny, but it was vandalized to hell. The Soviets should have remodelled it to make the fellow a smidge more popular. Perhaps a pose for the ages: entwined naked with Leonardo da Vinci, giving each other looks that say, "Four hundred years couldn't keep us apart. Can you believe it? Give me a kiss."

Didn't anyone think to tell the Soviets that if they wanted to engineer the human soul, they should start with the body?

In the Osiedle Sportowe housing complex on Ignacego Mościckiego Street, where I live, there are industrial smoke detectors on every floor. Smart. The Stalinists didn't want fires in the workers' paradise—fire, historically, has led to even greater trouble—so they planted them everywhere, like landmines. These hidden screamers catch Pani Laszkiewicz every time she goes for a smoke in the stairwell. The building fire alarm rings and a whole eastern bloc of cranky neigh-bours file past her. Some of these reluctant evacuees spit at her vinyl maid's shoes, others snap her cigarette in two, usually in mid-puff.

The building has a fire warden on every floor, entrusted with the task of saving lives. On each of their doors, there's a hulking brass knocker in case we have to wake them during the night. You can guess what the kids do for kicks, right? The smaller tots can't reach the knocker alone, so they build teetering human pyramids and clamber over each other to knock their floor-warden into a pissy mood.

Nowa Huta, a bottle's throw from Kraków, was designed as a planned community, but the plan makes no sense. We once had the biggest steel mill in the country, though Nowa Huta is hundreds of kilometres away from the nearest iron ore deposit. To build this town—a model for future sustainable living—workers bricked over the most fertile, nutrient-soaked land in the nation.

Sustaining ourselves here has sometimes meant tearing concrete slabs out of the earth to plant vegetable gardens.

This proves a point of mine: you have to destroy in order to create. I will not gum up progress. I would be the last one, I swear to you, to knock the fire warden awake. I believe that all fires have a purpose, and I'll tell you more about that later.

I forgot to remove my black nail polish before going to the urzędnik's office to pay my rent yesterday, and on the way, I ran into Pan Laskiewicz, the husband of secret smoker Pani Laskiewicz. As always, he went to shake my hand (but never in a doorway, of course, because that would be inviting bad luck), and he saw my nails. Pan Laskiewicz is like a saltwater sky: sunny one minute, and a spitting, Baltic hurricane the next. He snarls at the Poczta Polska when they fold his letters to fit them into the letterbox. He pretends to have good manners, but he's more like a wild boar in a human skin. A real son-of-an-asshole.

A funny look came over his face when he saw my black nails.

"That's my wife's," he said. "She's the only one who wears black on the end of her fingers." Even though it's his first language, Pan Laskiewicz's Polish wasn't very good. You could almost see, as one facial twitch ignited another, that he was piecing together a conspiracy in his head. "She adores young men like you, young bucks."

"What are you insinuating?"

"It doesn't take a pig brain to realize what you two are doing together," he said, reaching to fix the suspenders on my glue-spattered overalls. I couldn't tell if he was casing the best way to bowl me down the main hallway or if he had developed a new respect for me. His generation, it was rumoured, had a love-hate relationship with the young.

"Sorry to tell you," I replied, "but I don't find your wife attractive."

I felt lightning behind my eyelids, my face racing towards the sun. My mind caught up with reality, and I saw Pan Laskiewicz unclench his fist. He had boxed me squarely in the jaw. A corner of my lip exploded. I jumped him and we fell to the floor, the young and the old grappling for power, just like it had always been in Poland. I saw the opportunity to bite his ear off, but I whispered into it instead, caressing it with my lips.

"I am a homosexual," I said.

That was true, at least according to the broad-brush definition on Polish Wikipedia.

His grip on my balls relaxed and his hand fell away, almost thoughtfully. I started to breathe normally again.

"A cocksucker," I reiterated. "An expert in shopping for nail polish. And clearly, I am more physical with you than with your wife."

He rolled away and smiled at me. A slice of a smile. There were grumes of my blood on his fingertips.

"No. I still believe you two have been fucking, but that's okay." He flicked my ear affectionately, a macho zing. "I wouldn't be friends with a homosexual, so you're obviously making it up. Tell me, though, does she ... *arrive at full expression* with you?"

The janitor suddenly appeared and nonchalantly started to sweep the trash around us, brushing an ice cream sandwich wrapper noisily past our heads. Ants were making love to it.

I realized that I had lost. For I was fighting not a man who disliked homos but a whole country that refused to acknowledge we existed. Is there a point in standing up for yourself if you're invisible, if people will simply look right through you?

Now let's do a safety check.

Nowa Huta is full of smoke detectors, though they're blanketed with dust; even the newest ones would melt by the time smoke triggered the mechanism. Sure, the *administracja* appointed a fire warden for every floor, except they managed to pick all the vodka-hounds. Too sauced, I'm guessing, to tell an inferno from a good stiff one that pushes you over the edge.

There are other violations.

The evacuation plan isn't shared with new tenants, escape routes are mapped to interfere with rescue personnel—whose stairway is it, anyway?—and the dry chemical fire extinguishers are only charged to 170 psi.

In answer to my own question, there's always a point in standing up for yourself.

Don't make me light a match, because I will win this war of visibility. You can see fires and the queers who start them for kilometres, especially at night.

ÊTRE ET DURER

Kraków is crows, but it is also parkour, the fine art of moving from point K to point Z as quickly and efficiently as possible.

Imagine walking into a *cukiernia* in deepest summer and ordering a *pączek z marmolada*. Your order, it would seem, has disturbed a cluster of wasps who were feasting on the pastry, and through jelly-covered eyes they scowl at you, the enemy. You suddenly need to gain the most ground possible in the shortest period of time. You flap your arms, willing your shoulder blades to transform into wings and break through the skin of your back.

These are the things of fairy tales. Parkour is not.

You zoom out of the *cukiernia* and past the milk bar on Grodzka Street, and you perform a Cat Pass over an old woman selling cloves of garlic from a basket. Strive for the speed of sound. You have no time to waste, not with angry stingers coming to get you. The fence surrounding the Franciscan Church is no match for you and your Dash Vault. You tread lightly over the old bones in the cemetery.

The specialized parkour terminology doesn't matter, nor would a face full of wasp venom, in the end. What matters is that you're a free spirit, that you conquer the landscape of your city. This discipline—not sport, not sport—that has slowly leaked out of France and into the streets of Kraków will teach you to turn any physical or mental obstacle to ash.

Mind your language. Parkour is not "freerunning," the same way that Nintendo is not Sega and *zupa ziemniaczana* is not toilet water.

Race north along Bracka. Flip not, for this is no performance and there are no spectators. You're only trying to better yourself. Left on Gołębia at full tilt and prepare for your Jagielloński University Dyno. Sneakers rap against the classroom windows before you drop, thud, and roll. A young woman stares through the glass, her startle melting to a smile. This *passe muraille* will not splinter your kneecaps because you have learned to absorb, transfer, give in. You have learned to turn on a *grosz*, and the soles of your feet have memorized the warp and woof of the cobblestone.

You are one with the city.

Run fast enough, and you can jump over a herd of crows before they fly away.

Someone told me it's called a "murder" of crows, but that sounds like an urban legend.

If parkour were an Olympic sport, Kraków bagel carts would be standard equipment. You turn right on Szczepańska Street, and you spot, a hundred metres ahead, one of those steaming metal contraptions with fogged-up glass. Burnt sesame seeds roast in the open air. There is always a bit of smoke in Kraków.

But the vendor sees you coming and opens his retractable umbrella, giving your hurdle another two metres of height. At the very last second, you switch targets to a parked Polonez with a rusty roof.

There's only one move that can get you over safely, the Kash Vault: Kong Vault + Dash Vault. Don't get tripped up in semantics. Just make sure you push off with your hands at the beginning and at the end, and then keep-the-fuck running.

You're amazed at all the *szopka* lying around. Who creates these random nativity scenes, in front yards and tree hollows and window-sills, ornate little dioramas on street corners and littering the Rynek Główny? It can be very confusing to *traceurs*—parkour fanatics like you and I—to run past Bethlehem so many times in one day. If time has stopped in Kraków, then parkour has frozen it.

Interesting. Every time you jump a wall, you feel the crumble of plaster or the chipping of wood. There's not enough cement in old cities to protect them from an all-out fire. At least you know how to run.

You have long since lost the wasps, and you did it thirteen seconds quicker than your previous record. To a *traceur*, this can represent a lifetime of improvement. *Gratulacje*.

But you never did get that donut.

You've done well if you're back on Grodzka Street. Ground rule: responsible *traceurs* can always get back to where they started.

And remember, you're not Wonder Woman, you're just repeating equations:

The flying squirrel can't fly but can glide up to twenty-five metres by controlling its patagium, a furry skin parachute stretched from wrist to ankle. Its tail is an airfoil that stops it from smashing into treetops.

In the deserts of the southwestern United States, the *Crotalus cerastes* sidewinds over the dunes, leaving a trail of perfect letter Js in the sand. Snakes are wigged-out locomotives.

The mother-of-pearl moth caterpillar is a self-propelled wheel, touching its head to its tail and spinning downhill at 300 revolutions per minute, forty times its normal speed. *Backward*. Catch this pupa if you can.

Parkour, you see, has stolen from the best.

Now, sprint south to the greatest challenge of all, the Zamek Wawelski. You are approaching a medieval fantasy, a royal castle on a slice of land jutting into the lazily flowing strip of crystal known as the Wisła River. The Zamek is the centrepiece of Kraków. A reminder that this is one of the only large Polish cities that wasn't demolished in World War II.

But you can't see the Wisła. Between you and the water is a stone wall almost 700 years old, covered in pillowy, slippery ivy leaves, only a few metres tall in places. An evacuation slide, if you dare to use it. You'll land on grass, and your kneecaps will be fine.

But you never know. I'm a dabbler, not a professional—I just do it to impress the guys. In general, I avoid obstacles taller than three feet because I have a bum knee and I'm as graceful as a rhino.

Besides, I have no idea how to apply parkour philosophies in my life, the sign of a true practitioner. *Être et durer*: to be and to last. Most days, this seems like an impossible task.

CHICAGO

This miniature construction project seemed easy at first, but the tiny details are ballooning out of proportion.

There's no way I can replicate the 17,500 buildings that burned in the Great Chicago Fire of 1871. My popsicle stick supply isn't the problem—it's the restrictive 1.5 by 1.5-metre plywood foundation that's forcing me to pick and choose between apothecary, blacksmith, and barber shops. Vegetable market or opera house: how does one decide?

Pink Floyd is the perfect soundtrack for resurrecting a ruined city. My LP copy of *Atom Heart Mother* doesn't have a single scratch on it.

I'm lucky to be paid for my work, but there is a downside: the glue fumes. The ventilation in this gallery isn't very good, but I can't crack open a window because the wind could upset my whole operation. Besides, I don't want my fans peeking in before I'm finished—they can wait for the vernissage. If I had decided to build Chicago at home, I would've had even less privacy because Nowa Hutans are the nosiest bunch I know.

The plywood is now a grid of pencil marks, blueprints for a highly flammable city. I've seen Old Chicago from above, upside-down, and clean through its transparent middle. Someone has to build it, to stoke the old embers.

A few days ago, I realized how I fit into the geometry of the universe.

The fire tetrahedron is a pyramid, the union of four equilateral triangles glued together at the vertices. It's how all fires start. I rarely believe in universal absolutes—in fact, I usually detest them—but I can't question this one, especially since I'm such an integral part of it.

Triangle 1: Heat. Transferred by conduction, convection, or radiation. Dancing molecules, swirling liquid or gas, or the toasty vacuum of space.

Triangle 2: Fuel. The combustible greats, none of which I need to name. Anyhow, I'm more interested in rogue materials not supposed to burn.

Triangle 3: An oxidizer, like oxygen, chlorine, iodine, or peroxide. Make sure, unless you're prepared to accept the consequences, never to smoke when you're bleaching your hair.

Triangle 4: Chain reaction. Bingo. A catalyst has to bring these three triangles together, or else they're useless. The catalyst must be insistent—ergo, human—to ensure continuity, to press for a truly destructive flame. Someone has to flick the lighter, light the match, match the fire's intensity with their own will to keep it going. It's an act of violence, sure, but also of creation.

I feel so grounded at the bottom of this pyramid.

With this foolproof formula, fire doesn't need much time to accomplish its magic. The Great Chicago Fire lasted just twenty-seven hours, and managed to cut a swath of charred land across eight square kilometres of urban development and 120 kilometres of road.

I think I'm going to start with the Aragon Ballroom. It's a rectangular box relatively easy to re-create. Let's double up the popsicle sticks for thickness, to soundproof the walls. Big bands bray, and the brass section is a nightly riot. With surgical scissors, I can make everything fit.

There's a well-known legend about how this fire started. Perhaps you've heard it: Catherine O'Leary's milking cow kicked over a lantern in a hay-filled barn. The journalist who originally published this story later recanted, confessing that he made up the livestock angle to give the story some juice. But is it possible that O'Leary's cow actually *had* set Chicago ablaze, and that *the confession* was the attention grabber? What do you think?

At the risk of sounding like a conspiracy theorist, I'd like to stab this from a few angles, if you will permit.

The past and present members of Pink Floyd, I'm now certain, believe the cow story. Just look at the cover art for *Atom Heart Mother*. A Holstein cow is standing in a field—perhaps the band's vision of farm heaven—looking back inquisitively, as if to say, "Did I do that?"

Sure, sure, no direct link to Chicago. But when you probe a little deeper, it's clear that Pink Floyd are a bunch of pyros. Originally, before it was renamed, the title track on *Atom Heart Mother* was "The Amazing Pudding." Is it mere coincidence that the Great Fire of London in 1666 started in the bakery of Thomas Farynor on Pudding Lane?

And do you think the triangle on the *Dark Side of the Moon* album cover could be anything other than an homage to the fire tetrahedron? Please.

Chicago now needs my attention. I'll roll out the rest of my evidence a little later.

Before I put the roof on the Aragon, I'll need to make sure the bucket seats are lined up properly. And I've discovered that the glue warps the wood when it dries, so I'll need to prefabricate the seats with a C-clamp from now on, and then drop them in by finger crane just before showtime. The audience needs thumbnails of foam, of course, or they won't be entirely comfortable.

The Aragon marquee, in the 1:50 scale that I'm using to recreate this fire, is the exact size and shape of a single popsicle stick. I'll be able to paint the letters on a smooth, uninterrupted surface, and that brings me shards of peace. My fingers are infinitely happy. The tingle moves up.

It's kind of silly. Ever since humans learned the art of fire—yes, it's an art, not an obsession or a crime—we have been trying frantically to put it out. We're confirmed as the fourth triangle of an inseparable pyramid, yet some will spend their last kilojoule denying it, refusing to see that the only way to grow is to lose what's precious. Fire, bless its blue and white heart, does not choose indiscriminately. It wheedles out the weakest elements in the societies we build and forces us to do it better the next time. It's intelligent.

Nothing is fireproof. Anything will burn, if the fire is hot enough. And as long as it stays that way, we'll always be improving.

From the *Chicago Herald Tribune*, the week of the fire: "Cheer up! In the midst of a calamity without parallel in the world's history, looking upon the ashes of thirty years' accumulation, the people of this once beautiful city have resolved that Chicago shall rise again with vigor."

It did. The city bounced back, a frightening tangle of steel, glass, and concrete, each building striving not to be the weakest. By the time Chicago hosted the World's Fair just twenty-two years later, all the wood was gone. Lumber yards, elevated plank sidewalks, tinder bungalows packed with firewood—vanished.

One dude, however, failed to learn the beautiful lesson the fire had taught, calling his hotel the World's First Fireproof Building.

That really gets my sheep.

The record has finished, and I'm listening to the tinny thump of the inner groove. Now that I've finished the Aragon Ballroom, I have a confession to make: it was built in 1926, long after the Great Fire. Still, I couldn't resist putting it in my maquette.

Here's why.

The Ballroom was big-band headquarters for many years until a fire in a cocktail lounge next door—much smaller than in 1871, I assure you—forced Benny Goodman and other greats to play elsewhere. The theatre had a few false resuscitations after that, and eventually gained full strength as a rock venue. The apex? Pink Floyd played the Aragon Ballroom in 1970, the year they recorded *Atom Heart Mother*.

Now do you see what I mean about their pyromaniac tendencies? It sends shivers up my spine.

If you'll excuse me, it's getting late, and I have the rest of the city to erect.

Oh yeah, one more thing: if you think "Comfortably Numb" is Pink Floyd's best song, then you're a lightweight, but it's not your fault. Most people don't understand that you can't judge Floyd songs on their own, that concept albums don't exist in pieces.

THE LORD'S WORK

Nowa Huta, with its concrete monoliths buffered by patches of soggy grass and swollen bushes, with its metal railings sidling around corners and out of eyeshot, was made for parkour.

Built for a discipline that would come five decades later.

I remember when I first heard about this martial art creeping into Poland. It was a ghost element of our gradual entry into the European Union, gliding in on passports that became increasingly useless until, one day last year, they didn't need to be stamped anymore. I learned about parkour through a neighbour; more precisely, through the screams when his elbow shattered and bone fragments stuck into the grass, pinning his arm to the ground. I later learned that he had bent parkour's non-competition rules and had paid the price.

Quel dommage, as the French say.

The doctor who treated him wasn't very understanding of this new phenomenon because he forbade further practice. Even worse, the *administracja* installed barbed wire along the walls, railings, and concrete surfaces of Osiedle Sportowe, as if we were too stupid to injure ourselves elsewhere.

As if people don't eventually get what they want.

A bunch of us guys from Sportowe shrugged off danger and followed the lead of our friend without an elbow, although we obeyed the rules of parkour more rigidly than he did. As we conquered the physical world and bettered ourselves as human beings, we often pointed out each other's flaws: a flubbed *lâché*, a missed *demitour*, a downright embarrassing Underbar.

Self-improvement should be fun, but it rarely is.

The Underbar can go horrifyingly wrong. You start to pull yourself through a gap in the railing, but you get distracted. Perhaps it's a Lot Polish Airlines jet tearing the sky a new set of buttocks, but more likely it's the *urzędnik* storming toward you with a rent cheque you remember signing, but don't remember depositing enough money in the bank to cover.

Either way, you're screwed.

You misjudge your descent by a centimetre or two, and the steel bar wallops your chin. Your incisors punch holes in your tongue and you can't even pronounce the best cuss word in the language: *kurrrrrrrva*.

In the end, I got what I wanted and acquired a few scrapes of my own. Parkour, like many other forces in Poland, cannot be stopped.

But when the *urzędnik* came running after me, all red-faced and *zagniewane* and about to stuff a bounced cheque down my throat, I would run to the boiler room and lock myself in there, waiting for her to go away. Childish, yes, but parkour makes you a kid again.

It can make you horny, too. I used to fuck in that boiler room.

Karol, a hunk from my building, spent whole summers tempting me, walking around in a cut-off T-shirt that showed off his glorious armpit hair. Those puffs of pheromone candy beckoning me to sniff.

We would do it in the dark. He would be sitting with his back against the wall, his long, hairy legs splayed out in front of him. I would be sitting on his knees, slobbering over him, tasting the stinging sweat on his shoulders and hurting my lips on his stubble, jerking him off with one hand and swirling his spaghetti hair with the other. Somewhere in my sexual history, I had conceived the idea of giving my lovers a multimedia experience. They had to feel like they were in an MTV music video or in a car commercial, or it simply wasn't good sex. I still believe that.

Inevitably, the smell of his crotch would get to me, and I'd root out his testicles like a rutting pig. They hung several inches away from him like loosely attached eggs, as if on display. I smelled, licked, and sucked them. A kind of gender worship, I guess. I imagined piercing through the skin when he was least expecting it, siphoning out his testosterone with illicit sips, and then waiting for his pubic hair to sprout magically through my cheeks so I could smell him all day. Me, the lusty and deluded Chia Pet.

I am a swine, an alchemist, a human. I am a curious boy of twenty-five.

One of those times, Karol was most rude.

"Radek, I would like to see you naked."

"*Je ne comprends pas.*" I had already begun to speak the language of the revolution.

"Don't be coy when I'm horny," he said. "That just makes me frustrated." He put his hand behind my head, yanked it like a slot machine handle, and I went down. Choked on pre-cum. I loved the feeling of his cock head stretching the back of my throat. It changed how I spoke, ever so slightly, giving my vowels a hollow touch.

"But I like it when you're frustrated," I said. "It makes you do things to me."

I stood up, shucked my shorts, and instantly heard the voice of the apostle Paul, residual ramblings from somewhere in my childhood.

> Do you not know that the unrighteous will not inherit
> the kingdom of God? Do not be deceived; neither forni-
> cators, nor idolaters, nor adulterers, nor the effeminate,
> nor homosexuals, nor thieves, nor the covetous, nor
> drunkards, nor revilers, nor swindlers will inherit the
> kingdom of God.

I was not made for the Lord's work. I was built for fucking, and I had known that for many years. But these scriptures echo across the land, and it's hard to tune them out completely, to escape even subtle pangs of guilt. I had Karol's stinky pubes in my teeth, his fingers near my shitty hole, and the stain of dried DNA on my belly; I processed these stimuli through years of programming and filters that told me the body was an unclean organism that worms its way closer to hell every day. Fail, fail, fail.

You cannot outrun echoes in Poland, but you can block them out. There are ways to loosen the church's grip on your crotch.

Karol cupped my ass, perhaps to catch my sway, perhaps to centre my asshole over his cock so it would be a clean pierce when I eventually squatted.

I recoiled from his touch.

"What's wrong?" he said.

"Maybe we can do it with my clothes on."

"Are you retarded?"

"Don't be a hater," I said.

"How is sex even possible with your clothes on?"

In a way, clothing had protected me from sin though many sound fuckings: if my body was only a remote participant, then it wasn't exactly sex.

"My jeans have holes in all the right places."

24

I was ready to defy the apostle Paul with a striptease for the ages, but Karol was already zipping up.

"Someday," he said, "we're going to need you to fuck openly." He pulled an elastic band around his pony tail. "We might all have to fuck in the streets until people get it. No more hiding."

Sure. I was conquering the physical world, all right.

DANISH BLUE

Chicago hardly fit through the doors of Kraków's No. 8 tramwaj, but the driver let me force it through and chip the corners where future suburbs would grow. He knew that the incredible level of detail would keep the kids from screaming for a few stops.

I couldn't reach the timestamp to validate my green transit ticket. This happens every now and then. *Jaka szkoda.* If the ticket-taker ever catches me, I'll just bribe him with a free tour of Chicago's Magnificent Mile. I don't know what the Communists were thinking, putting Polish trams on the honour system. As if we wouldn't figure out, after all these years, how to ride with an unstamped ticket.

An oak tree uprooted and fell off into a woman's handbag without her knowing. She had such a stern face, I decided not to retrieve it.

I got off at Stradom station and paid some guy two złotych to help me carry the maquette to the nearby Człowiek Obcy Gallery. My original gallery—the one that had commissioned this doomed artifact— had gotten nervous about my plans for the exhibition. They said I was *zwariowany,* but you have to be that way to make art that plants razor blades in the gums.

That's the thing. We all want art to hurt us, but only through the screams of others.

In the space behind the gallery, the director had thoughtfully erected four cinderblock pillars waist-high on which I could lay Chicago.

I prepared the materials I needed for my performance, and by the time I was done, the wine-and-cheese was in full roar. Danish blue cheese and cheap, Hungarian swill for wine. Nearly everybody was dressed in Dolce & Gabbana, looking like appetizers. The Jagielloński University crowd never missed a show at Człowiek Obcy, though they couldn't care less who the artist was. This was their social mandate— to support non-university trouble-making, no matter what it was, so they could criticize the *akademia* with some credibility.

They were most welcome to my show.

A girl—you know what I mean, a woman—was reciting Czesław Miłosz to her friends. It's easy to appear pretentious when quoting this writer, but she was choosing unknown passages, or at least ones not repeated to death. Her listeners didn't applaud; they fell silent.

Her hair was long and licorice black, her skin pale beneath the curls. Sarcastic eyes. Does that make sense? I liked her instantly.

Clap, clap, clap. The director wanted our attention. He was dressed in a bow tie and smoking jacket, hair flattened with Brylcreem. You could tell it was meant to be ironic. I was wearing my favourite pair of blue overalls. My busted lip had more or less healed.

"*Uwaga, uwaga, panie i panowie!* The artist is ready to commence the performance. Please give a hand to S. Mok Wawelski, and move outside to the courtyard."

I use an artist name. Gotta problem with that? Radek Tomaszewski is as ordinary as kielbasa and Żywiec beer, and not destined to attract attention, so I had to choose something flashier.

I stood on the east side of Chicago, where Lake Michigan would be, where many had jumped into the water to save themselves from the flames and smoke. The students gathered around, lazily drinking their wine and smoking West cigarettes.

"Thank you for coming," I said. "This is what Chicago looked like on the morning of October 8, 1871. You'll see that everything was made of wood. They ate a lot of ice pops."

Laughter. Someone raised their hand.

"How many people died?"

"That depends on which account you believe," I said. "Humans are always the most poorly documented factors in a tragedy. I could tell you three hundred, but that wouldn't be counting paperless immigrants, the poor, or the homeless."

"Or queers," lit girl said, smiling. Her teeth were stained red by wine.

"True," I said, and bookmarked her for later. This may sound strange, but I wanted to see her take a piss. I occasionally get curious about women, and it's usually precipitated by quirky behaviour like hers. "Now step back."

I picked up a can of butane.

"Where's the artist statement?" someone said.

Sigh. Purists. I had been dreading this moment; I've never been comfortable summarizing my work. It's so reductive. You can't explain away a conflagration or what it means. Sky-high flames, searing heat, and suffocating smoke make different impressions on each of us. Fire alters your micro-climate in ways inexplicable to others.

For my statement, I chose to stick to the facts.

"Fireproofing is a myth," I said. "The biggest one since 'the immortality of the soul.'"

I squirted streams of butane over the Gold Coast, the Loop, Streeterville, and a bunch of other neighbourhoods. The Chicago Water Tower was one of the few structures in the burn zone that remained standing in the fire, and I was determined to change that.

After all, this was my chance to tinker with history.

I lifted a fire extinguisher to the audience, who were getting noticeably nervous. Gulping their wine.

"Take note that this extinguisher has been emptied. The waterworks broke down during the Great Fire. We will deal with a similar disadvantage."

Showtime. I stood back, lit a match, and threw it over the city. Orange and blue flames ignited in the downtown sky. Fire dripped down to the land and flowed like lava over the landscape until it was an even, vibrating carpet of light. Glue melted and poured into the streets, and popsicle sticks snapped and blackened. Wind blew the smoke northward into the faces of the guests, and many of them ran toward me where they could breathe. Some scampered into the gallery. The flames were almost as high as a nearby clothesline, three, maybe four metres, colouring the clouds from our point of view. It was a bit much.

In the crackling, whistling wood, I could hear the echoes of human screams from 1871, drowned out by primitive fire alarms, bells rung by hand. Some sounds just seem to go together, or maybe it's just me.

"We have a problem," the director called to me, emerging from the gallery.

He was followed by six strażaków lumbering in Nomex and Kevlar suits and toting axes, fire hoses, and an extinguisher the size of a small beer fridge.

"Przenieść się!"

We obeyed and moved out of the way while they blew dry chemicals over Chicago, clouding its skies and coating the streets with an eerie off-white powder. The fire was reduced to smouldering ash. A giant hole had burned away where City Hall was; municipal hell was a pit of blackened sodium bicarbonate that ended at the grass.

"Who is responsible for this?" one of the firefighters asked. The big one.

"*S'il vous plaît n'hésitez pas à gouter le fromage,*" I told him. "The grapes are good, too."

"Your French is impeccable," lit girl told me. "My name is Dorota."

"The department never authorized this show," he said. "We're shutting you down."

"What about you?" I said, showing him the stopwatch I kept handy, anticipating his visit. "It took you six minutes and thirty-two seconds to get here. That's far past the national average of five minutes."

"I could have you arrested for public endangerment—like this." He snapped his fingers.

He looked peeved and maybe a little horny. I detected vapours of potato and bison grass on his breath; bootlegged vodka almost always means "party-time." I pictured the gang of them punishing me by stuffing a fire hose up my ass. The fantasy was all right, as long as they didn't loosen the valve ...

Dorota stepped through the ranks of the crowd—now shrunken to a gossipy whisper—and moseyed over with her glass of wine. Swish. She was mesmerizing.

"You know, Radeki isn't the only one who broke the rules. You entered what you knew was a burning building without attaching a lifeline to your belts."

"Radeki." My birth name is Radosław, though I use the diminutive form "Radek." She had just made my name even more kid-like.

The *strażaków* looked down at their waists, dumbfounded, except for the boss. He stared straight at her and smirked.

"That is not your business, woman."

"Listen, we didn't mean to cause trouble," I said. "There will be no more fires."

"Radeki, don't be gutless. This man is a nincompoop, an idiot, a *bestia*. He didn't even bring floor plans of the building. If we were all dying and choking in smoke, these supposed 'firefighters' wouldn't have been able to save us." Now she addressed them, her eyes showing contempt. "Go home, and don't tell anyone what happened. You will be too embarrassed."

She was the ideal warrior: knowledgeable, fearless, an ass of sculpted glass. I realized on the spot that we could accomplish great things together, as long as I didn't ruin it by requesting a blowjob.

The big firefighter poked my forehead with his finger. "You are a marked man."

The *strażaków* left and so did about half the crowd. My true fans remained. The shaken director handed out plastic glasses and opened a bottle of champagne.

"*Gratulacje!*" he said. "I'll probably get an official reprimand for this, but it was worth it."

"Applause for Dorotka," I said, returning the diminutive.

Later, after she and I had downed a few bottles of Veuve Clicquot and *piwo jasne*, and had talked about school, art, politics, the Pope's floundering white blood cells, and the dark days ahead, she pulled a sheet of paper from her pocket.

"It's by Czesław Miłosz." She read it to me.

> At the entrance, my bare feet on the dirt floor, Here, gusts
> of heat; at my back, white clouds. I stare and stare. It
> seems I was called for this: To glorify things just because
> they are.

"What is that from?" I said.

"Fucked if I know ... but the old fart just died, so I figured it was appropriate."

"Harsh."

"His work is good, but I'm sure he was a rat, like the rest of us."

Just so you know, Człowiek Obcy, the name of the gallery, means "outsider." I know Polish is confusing, but please try to keep up.

YOUTUBE

May Day 1983, Warszawa

Black screen.

They gather in the Old Town. The crowd slowly thickens with bodies as people stream through the archway like meat through a sausage machine. Zoom in on a man with glasses, batting away the red and white *Solidarność* flag. He can't see. There is nothing to see yet. The crowd is too calm.

Zoom out. The young are dressed in red and white, the colours of the revolution. The old are wearing grey or blue or beige. They want the revolution, but it will not disrupt their dressing routines. Nor should it.

Static.

All Poland is with us.

The crowd begins to chant. Out of focus, a man with a moustache echoes the words a split second before we hear them. He gets hit by a white balloon, but we don't see who has thrown it. Perhaps a child.

Nie ma wolności bez Solidarności.

Nie ma wolności bez Solidarności.

No freedom without Solidarity.

The camera zooms out a bit too far, then readjusts. There are many balloons, only they are not balloons but white rubber batons the police are flailing. A woman falls to the ground as the police beat people back through the archway. The batons sometimes bounce back, like in a cartoon, but the officers are wearing helmets with visors to protect themselves. From themselves. The fallen woman collects the contents of her purse on the cobblestone. We see a change holder for *grosze* and keepsakes. One of her high heels is broken. It lays dismembered at her side.

We want the truth.

They are inchoate, but everyone knows what the other is starting to say. Words they never thought possible. Never thought Polish.

We want the truth.

The visors are smoke-coloured. The police always see smoke and never know when it's real.

A stampede. The crowd crushes through the stone gate. Solidarity flags coil around them like taffy. Blinding and tripping them. The camera fixes on officers beating their riot shields. An old man approaches them, shaking his fist.

All Poland is with us.

All Poland is wet. Water everywhere. The police turn hoses full blast on the crowd who cannot escape fast enough. The water hammers their heads. Their hair is soaked and matted, and their faces turn purple. They look like newborn babies, but this is not yet a new country.

A stampede. The crowd crushes through the stone gate. Solidarity flags coil around them like taffy. Blinding and tripping them. The tape loops. We see the same activities. It is always the same.

All Poland is with us.

We want the truth.

Try chanting with water spraying the back of your throat. See how it feels.

Nearly all the demonstrators have left. Zoom in on an old woman who remains. The old remain the longest. It is their nature. In Poland, "old" is not a bad word.

She is the brightest of all in a crimson cardigan. She is holding her hands over her ears to block out the mayhem. She must hear far more than we do. The riot police approach. Another woman—a younger one—pleads with her, tries to pull her hands off her ears. But the old woman's arms have locked. The younger one pulls and pulls. One gnarled hand comes loose, hesitates in the air.

The country waits.

Blood comes out of the old woman's ear. She was trying to hold it in all this time. She just didn't know what side was bleeding.

Nobody knows which side is bleeding more.

All Poland is with us.

We want the truth.

You fucking bastards.

Fade to black.

Cut to red and white.

CMENTARZ

The *herbatka* was bitter, just how we like it. Tea should never be a sweet affair.

Dorota sat in an armchair in the corner of my one-room studio apartment (millionaire I am not). She sipped her tea at intervals of exactly thirty seconds, surreptitiously watching me dress. I know when I'm being watched, a talent that has served me well in life.

She was reading a copy of *Rzeczpospolita* abandoned by the neighbours. The older folks in my building have given up on the national newspaper. They gripe that ever since Poland joined the EU the year before, the paper has become a political hand puppet. They don't cancel their subscriptions, because there's no refund policy in Poland; "bought" is bought. So copies pile up in my building entranceway and get mashed to a pulp by wet galoshes. Unless I read them.

I am a good tenant. I help clean up and digest the weekly tidbits before they're completely illegible.

Rarely did I let anyone into my personal space. I thought about dismantling my Pink Floyd shrine before Dorota arrived (no one else had ever seen it), but in the end, I resisted the urge. It would be too complicated to reassemble and, besides, I wanted her to know more about me.

It was typical, as far as shrines go:

LP albums arranged left to right according to the band members' favourites, starting with the most senior musicians

Papier-mâché models of the inflatable pig that floated loose during the *Animals* album cover shoot, suspended from my ceiling with threads of varying length, marking the ascent

Fan photos of reclusive founding member Syd Barrett transporting quarts of milk in the basket of his banana-seat bicycle

A re-creation of *The Wall*, made of real bricks, with the middle one missing and a picture of my face peeking through

She didn't say a word about this stuff, even though it took up half a wall directly across from where she was sitting near the balcony.

My black jeans had faded to off-black and no longer matched my T-shirt. I never had this problem with my beloved corduroy overalls, but the evening's activities called for a change of wardrobe. Dorota continued to watch me.

"I can't go out like this," I told her. "Can I try on your pants?"

Dorota put her newspaper down, maintaining her ruse of being absorbed in reading. "Yes, you 'haven't got a stitch to wear,' just like Morrissey. Very cute. Just hurry up and tuck that sausage into whatever will hold it."

"Do you like men or women?" I asked her. A point-blank kind of gal would have no qualms with a direct hit like this.

"I like body parts. Guys, mostly, but different people have the parts I like. I'm attracted to the ones who show them off. What kind of question is that, anyways?"

"I just want to know more about you."

"Interrogating me isn't going to help you. But I know you mean well."

"Doesn't seem that weird to me ... a really cool person walks into my life and I want to ask a few questions."

"You're talking too much." She melted a bit in her chair, and gave me a smile I'll never forget. "And actually, sweetie, you walked into my life. I was going to that gallery years before you even knew about it."

Dorota continued reading and her smile faded. She pulled a pair of surgical scissors out of her purse and snipped out a rectangle of newsprint, violently crumpling the rest of the section and throwing it—unknowingly, I hoped—at my rare Dutch pressing of *Dark Side of the Moon*.

"Listen to this," she said with a sneer, reading from the newspaper. "'If deviants begin to demonstrate, they should be hit with batons ... a couple of baton strikes will deter them from coming again. Gays are cowards by definition.'"

"And what hero of ours said this?"

"Wojciech Wierzejski, Deputy of the Polish National Assembly. I'll add it to the collection."

"You have more?"

"An endless supply," she said.

We finished our *herbatka* in silence. I was soon done fussing over my outfit.

We got off the *tramwaj* at Rakowicki Cemetery, and walked through the gates just after midnight. I felt a *frisson*. This was the Euro Disney of cemeteries, a necropolis. Death is done right in Poland, and I don't mean that with any disrespect. I mean that angels are sculpted of marble, not granite, tombs are kept clean and accessible, the catacombs and columbariums pristine. Corpse names are written in fonts so sexy they make you want to cum. The architecture of remembrance is not left to lie fallow, not here. The parents of Pope Jan Paweł II were buried here, but that wasn't why we'd made the trip.

Dressing in black to visit a cemetery is cliché, but when the purpose of your visit is to candle-bomb the place, it's just practical. Stealth is prime in such situations.

Dorota carried the candles in a burlap sack, and I brought my lighter of choice. For our first gentle act of terror we chose the grave of Helena Modrzejewska, a female theatre star who, as not many people know, had occasionally played men onstage. She had fucked with the order of things, and now we would, too.

"You write. I'll light," I said.

Dorota placed the cylindrical, windproof candles like widely-spaced dominoes, taking her time to form the letters. I gave them life. When she was redoing the elbow of a K, I noticed how the light carved shadows into the hollows of her face, making her look like a Jack-o'-Pumpkin. I was following her too closely to read the words (I was a little scared, so stayed close for protection).

"Windproof" is about as solid a concept as "fireproof." On that breezeless night, I managed to blow a bunch of candles out with my excited talking. "How long do these candles last? Will they be visible by daylight? We should be taking pictures. Next cemetery!"

When we had finished the first word, Dorota laughed like a crazy *żabka* and hugged me close, pressing her mouth to my neck. I was about to put her into a playful headlock, but she grabbed my hand

and ran. We tore through the obstacle course of *nagrobeks*, tripping over ivy tentacles and kicking flower planters like footballs, blind in the dark but headed, our ankles told us, toward higher ground. We were sinning, and it was delicious.

We turned around to see Helena's grave, lit up prettily by Dorota's imagination and my steady hand:

SUCK THIS DEVIANT COCK IN THE INTERMISSION

Cemeteries usually only saw mass candle activity on All Souls' Day, a compulsive keening for the dead you might recognize as Halloween. That was months away, so we knew our texts wouldn't get drowned by other lights. Our accents would flicker crisply, and I hoped this activity would lead to bigger fires together.

"Who's next?" I said.

"You mean which dead body?"

"Which bigoted asshole."

She reached into her purse, slung across her torso commando-style, and fished out a swatch of news clippings.

"Take your pick," she said. "Either 'homosexual practices lead to drama, emptiness, and degeneracy,' or 'if a person tries to infect others with their homosexuality, then the state must intervene in this violation of freedom.' I'm leaning toward the second one, because it's from Kazimierz Marcinkiewicz. The prime minister."

"The first one is more poetic," I said.

"But the prime minister is a swine."

"Art before activism."

"You're impossible," Dorota said.

We found a magnificent tomb encased in green moss. This time I chose the wording (rather long, and taxing on the lumbar muscles), and Dorota lit the candles. The firelight eroded a bit of the cemetery's soft, sepulchral charm, sharpening moon shadows into right angles. You can't get anywhere, I reminded myself, without disturbing the peace.

Radeki. Dorotka. Using diminutive names was the hot, new trend. I was sure the prime minister would accept our raspberry kisses:

KASIO, BE NICE TO US. DON'T BE A DRAMA QUEEN

Cemeteries are made for parkour. Yes, that's what I said about Nowa Huta and Kraków, but this time I really mean it.

Tombstones make the perfect hurdles, especially if commissioned by a poor family (not too high). Some of them are staggered diagonally in Rakowicki, so there's enough room to Breakfall after you clear one. Although it gets a lot more fun when a security guard is chasing you.

We got lucky.

"Ditch the candles," I said to Dorota. "You'll be able to run faster and focus on your movements. Just follow my lead."

We performed lazy vaults over unimposing stones, but had to switch to time-consuming *sauts de précision* when we ran into old money, a minefield of graves so big I almost twisted my ankle in the inscription letters. Even so, we put a comfortable fifty metres between ourselves and the guard.

"*Idź do diabła!*" he screamed at us, giving up the chase when he reached a fence too high to jump.

"That's funny," I said. "We're going to hell anyways."

The glory of parkour was leaving people like him, folks who don't know the body language of freedom, behind.

We stopped running, however, when we saw sprays of light

illuminating the grass in front of us, and turned around. Back at the crime scene, the bastard was kicking over all our hard work, jumbling the letters, rendering our messages wonky and dyslexic. The security guard wasn't the target of our messages; we had bigger *ryby* to fry. I hadn't planned for this kind of failure.

Dorota held out the bag of candles.

"You didn't get rid of those, like I told you?"

"I'm not sure why you think I should listen to you," she said. "And just so you know, Pink Floyd isn't that good. They write okay songs but the instrumental solos are ... well, too long."

"I'll pretend I didn't hear that."

We spelled our last fragment of the night. It wasn't our best, but I went to bed hoping it would crawl across the country on the lips of the disobedient and the curious:

SOLIDARITY FOR POLISH QUEERS

VERMICULITE

Thank you for visiting the Vermiculite Association website.

[No, thank you. Pictured is a rock with a glassy face that looks suspiciously like magnetite or obsidian after a dandruff shampoo and molecular combover. Thoroughly unconvincing.]

Vermiculite is the mineralogical name given to hydrated laminar magnesium-aluminum-iron silicate.

When subjected to heat, vermiculite has the unusual property of exfoliating, or expanding into wormlike pieces. It is used to make fire protection materials, insulation, ovens, brake pads, acoustic finishes, sound-deadening compounds, seedling wedge mixes, fertilizer, and animal feed.

[Expanding animal feed. Hmmm. Maybe that's how Mrs O'Leary's cow got so fat and klutzy.]

Vermiculite is one of the safest, most unique minerals in the world.

[A vermiculite mine in Libby, Montana was closed in 1990, after it was discovered to be contaminated with asbestos. While in operation, it supplied most of the vermiculite used in the construction of thirty-five million homes across America, in the form of the supposedly fireproof Zonolite Masonry Insulation. Cough, cough. Cancer's in the attic. And in those cookies you baked.]

It is lightweight and non-combustible.

[Big lie. Vermiculite can most certainly burn. It can only withstand temperatures of up to 1,100°C—far cooler than a natural gas flame (1,250°C), a blowtorch flame (1,300°C), or an oxyhydrogen inferno (2,000°C). You want your house to incinerate? Build it with "fire-proof" material. Drizzle vermiculite around your bedposts and say a hex. I invite skeptical scientists out there to spend an educational afternoon with me.]

Our objective is to promote wider use and increased consumption of vermiculite-based products.

[Wish us all luck.]

CHOCOLATE MILK

I would've been a likelier candidate as a janitor or football mascot than as a visiting speaker at Universytet Jagielloński, one of the world's most revered educational facilities. I've learned, however, to accept life's injustices with a smattering of grace.

By the way, when I say "football," I mean "soccer."

There was no way to turn down Dorota's invitation to present to her fellow art history students without pissing her off. Besides, the gig paid 100 złotych, rent was due any day, and I didn't want to get into another tiff with the *administracja*.

For that price, I came with black nail polish.

"What do you want me to talk about?" I asked Dorota. We had arrived in class ahead of the other students. I knew nothing about art history.

"Don't worry, they'll ask lots of questions," she said with a wink. "They're an inquisitive bunch. This is a remedial class, so there are clueless students from all disciplines."

"Literature, too?"

"You're looking at her."

"I didn't mean it that way," I said, embarrassed. "I've been meaning to ask you ... are you writing poetry, or just studying it?"

"Is there a difference?"

"I guess not," I said.

"Radeki, don't let me be an asshole to you," she said, laughing. "I'm experimenting right now, and I'm not ready to show you anything yet."

"I just want you to remember that I'm terrible at judging poetry. I'll love even what you hate."

Once the class had filled in and everyone had taken their seats, the professor gave Dorota a piece of chalk, the cue to introduce me.

"I want you to remember this name," she said to the class, scrawling S. MOK WAWELSKI on the blackboard. Whiteboards were not Ivy League enough for Jagielloński. "Please give him a warm welcome." She gave me the chalk.

After lukewarm applause, I sat on the corner of the professor's desk but tried not to give too much of a ball show; my overalls had shrunk in the dryer the night before.

"What do you know about me?" I asked, casting my line into a room I felt knew too much.

"You keep the fire department busy," a student said, getting a rise from the class. He was a redhead, arms covered with strawberry down. "Can you tell us about your influences?"

"Pink Floyd."

The professor shot Dorota a warning look worth 100 złotych and maybe more.

"I meant what miniaturists do you admire?"

"Uh, none," I said, taking advantage of the resulting silence to take a sip from my one-litre carton of chocolate milk.

"So you've never heard of the Beckonscot model village, the one with the burning house?" pressed the redhead, wrinkling the freckles on his nose. "I find it weird you don't acknowledge precedents for your work."

"*The Wall* is a great album, and if you listen carefully, it'll teach you all you need to know about building and tearing down."

Of course I studied precedents, but he was thinking miniature, and I tend to go oversize. For me, art history is about Christo and Jeanne-Claude unleashing their epic whims on the earth, visible from outer space. It's about having the gumption to hang a 14,000 m² orange curtain across the Rifle Gap Valley in the Rocky Mountains, to change the planet's very *topografía* at your vernissage. You can't think small without thinking large, but that wasn't a very academic thought, so I kept it to myself.

Another student raised her hand.

"What concerns does your practice raise regarding safety and personal space?"

"I don't know ... I mean, you can prepare for a fire your whole life, but it will always get you, because you can never think of everything. You know? At least once a year, you'll leave Kleenex near a heater, and you'll forget to turn off a stove burner. You can never protect your valuables, because you won't know what's important to you until you see its edges curling in a house fire."

I found it surprising that nobody, in this room full of pretentiati in training, asked me about my artist name.

Dorota winked at me.

I suddenly realized that my invitation to this class was an act of sabotage on the school. I winked back. It was time to have a bit of fun.

But first, you need to know more about Christo and Jeanne-Claude.

Husband and wife, environmental artists. They were both born on June 13, 1935, at the same hour. As part of their 1961 honeymoon (which, you might say, lasted decades), they created one of their first Low Art monuments by barricading the docks of Cologne, Germany with an oil-drum simulation of the Berlin Wall, to the bemusement of police and the horror of the art establishment.

Christo and Jeanne-Claude never flew together, so that if one died in a plane crash, the other could carry on with their work.

They remodelled Germany more than once. In 1995, they petitioned the 662 parliamentary delegates who had offices in the Berlin Reichstag, writing personalized letters and making phone calls asking for permission to wrap the building in "fireproof" polypropylene fabric. The delegates acquiesced after a seventy-minute debate on the parliament floor, and then Christo and Jeanne-Claude, with the help of hundreds of workers, threw a giant condom over them.

The German parliamentarians had reason to be nervous. The Reichstag had burned in 1933, and an enraged Hitler, convinced it was an act of arson by the Communist Party, manoeuvred to erase them from government. The Nazis then achieved a majority in the Reichstag, and eventually, single-party rule.

Maybe those 662 delegates knew that a fire could happen again, at any time.

All this. These two artists. But why would I reveal my true heroes to this class? I could just whisper their names into Dorota's ear some other time.

Dorota raised her hand, drawing a second stern glance from the professor. High Art, it was clear, was under assault.

"Young lady," I said.

"Is your art sexual?"

"Please explain," I said, blowing bubbles in my chocolate milk through the extendable straw.

"Czesław Miłosz once said in an interview that in his poems, 'You will find a very erotic attitude towards reality, towards simple things:

amazement, for instance, for the innumerable and boundless sub-stance of the earth—the scent of pine, the hue of fire, the white frost, the dance of cranes.' I was wondering if you feel the same way about your art."

"Art does not use the language of department-store perfume," I said. "But seriously, has it never bothered you that Miłosz put history and politics ahead of literary merit?"

"He had no choice," Dorota volleyed back. "Do you know what country this is?"

"The artist always has a choice."

"Not when his best friends are being imprisoned and assassinated."

"Okay. Good point."

The professor took the piece of chalk away from me and was about to call off the class, but strawberry boy raised his hand.

"Where did you graduate, Mr Wawelski?" he asked sarcastically.

"Funny you should ask," I said. "Jagielloński kicked me out a few years ago for a conversation almost exactly like this." I turned to the professor. "Do you pay cash, or will you be mailing me a cheque?"

Too bad they'll never hear my real artist statement, a bone that Christo tossed to a journalist over continental breakfast: "I think it takes much greater courage to create things to be gone than to create things that will remain."

Dorota and I left together. She cut her remaining classes for the day.

"You're not angry at me, are you?" I asked. "For the Miłosz stuff."

"No, not really. I'm too preoccupied by what you said about Kleenex and stoves. I'm afraid to ask you about your life and what happened to you. What you know."

"Don't worry. It'll come out one day."

"In the meantime, I'll try not to interrogate." She took my hand.

Her wrist was covered in goosebumps.

"Why did you do it?" I asked her. "Why did you want me to fuck with them? Don't get me wrong, it was amazing, but how did you know I would catch on?"

"I didn't. But I need somebody in my life who doesn't have to be told what to do, and I need them to see that none of this matters." She gestured to the walls I routinely scaled in fits of parkour. I wondered if she had ever seen my sneakers rapping on the glass. "Or maybe I'm the one who needs to see that. But you were more than amazing today. You were *ekstra*."

"And if I had failed? What if I had impressed them with shit about the intersection of urban planning, miniature cities, and world art?"

"Then I would have dropped you and found another friend," she said with no trace of jest. "Anyway, you don't know about that stuff, so what does it matter?"

GEMELLI HOSPITAL

[The Holy Father, Pope Giovanni Paolo II, was taken to Gemelli Hospital this Thursday, February 24, for a routine tracheotomy to ease his breathing. The operation proceeded according to schedule and was a success, and he sends his well-wishes to all of Rome.]

Dr Krzysztof Mazurkiewicz, emergency surgeon:

4:26 pm
After ensuring the patient's comfort, we identified the Jackson's triangle near the suprasternal notch, and injected a solution of lingocaine and adrenaline to minimize potential bleeding. We disinfected the area from the mandible to the sternum, and pre-lubricated the tracheal tube. A tapered and curved Cook model was chosen, to reduce the risk of damage to the tracheal wall. The Cook model is shaped like a rhino horn.

[His Eminence is evidently in jovial spirits, and was making jokes shortly after 8 pm. He directed that no general anaesthesia be used, and his wishes were respected.]

4:30 pm
Pay close attention, in case you have to do this yourself one day. We made an incision between the suprasternal notch and the cricoid

cartilage, and dissected the tissue with a cat's paw retractor. You cannot imagine the pressure of performing these tasks on such an important patient.

[It is not unusual for the Pope to visit the hospital more than once a month for health monitoring. He catches colds, as all Romans do. We are praying for his full recovery, and by all accounts, His Holiness has bounced back rather quickly.]

4:55 pm

Once the tracheal rings were visible, and after cauterizing the bleeding, we made a second incision between the second and third rings. Upon reaching this stage, it is ridiculously easy to "make a mistake." It is common knowledge that the price of making a medical mistake on this patient is instant removal from the premises. And execution.

[We might remind the media that the Holy Father has been an avid athlete all of his life, and that he has built up a natural resilience to "hiccups" of the body. He sends his love to the faithful in Poland, and says energetically that he "will see you all very soon."]

5:12 pm

Unfortunately, the patient continued to bleed in the epidermis from the first incision, with blood leaking into the trachea. This is common in older patients, but there was a man in the operating room known to conceal a pistol, so I cauterized again, even though over-cauterization could have led to complications ...

[Doctors report that never has a patient made such a quick recovery.]

5:14 pm

The bleeding stopped, but my staff was still nervous. I knew they had all rehearsed suicide routines in case anything went wrong. We injected a two percent silocaine solution into the tracheal incision to prevent cough. I hadn't performed a tracheotomy in a while, but the pistol brought back much of my medical training, as I knew it would. For example, I remembered that tracheotomies are actually called tracheostomies. When did we start forgetting the s? A Vatican doctor in the room reminded us that the patient's breathing still sounded difficult and that we needed to hurry up.

[What better time to buy His Eminence's latest book, *Memory and Identity: Conversations at the Dawn of a Millennium*, released this past Wednesday in hardcover by Rizzoli Press?]

5:17 pm
We inserted the tracheostomy tube and confirmed its position by holding a piece of gauze in front of the nozzle; it fluttered with every inhale and exhale, indicating that the patient's breathing had become more regular with the device in place. I pressed my thumb on the hole to feel the alternating blow and suction, just to be sure. I blocked the Holy Father's breathing for a few eternal seconds, and couldn't help but feel supernatural. His jugular was so, so close. We inflated the balloon cuff with air.

[From the critics: "The world will remember Pope John Paul II for espousing many of the convictions he expresses here: that good is ultimately victorious, life conquers death, and love triumphs over hate." —*Amazon.com*]

5:28pm
We performed two sutures to secure the tracheal tube to the Pope's skin, and then taped the free ends of the suture wire to his chest.

His Holiness has a preference for Polish doctors, which is why I was chosen. But if the man with the pistol had discovered I was homosexual, would he have shot me right there, or would he have taken the time to drag me outside into the *piazza*?

[Once his Holiness makes a full recovery, if he has not done so already by the grace of God and the Holy Virgin Mary, he will give Mass in Piazza San Pietro. We look forward to hearing the warmth and vigour in his voice once again.]

["He says of pro-choice and gay marriage advocacy that 'it is ... necessary to ask whether this is not the work of another ideology of evil, more subtle and hidden, perhaps, intent upon exploiting human rights themselves against man and against the family.'" —*Village Voice*]

5:30 pm

I did it.

It is known that someone who saves the life of the Pope on the operating table is guaranteed an early retirement with a *casa signorile* in the Alps, paid for by the state. In the span of an hour, I rose to the top of my profession and secured comfort for the rest of my life.

But I do not want it. This is what I want: a traditional Polish wedding with hundreds of friends and family, a giant cake made of *serek*, and "*sto lat*" and "*na zdrowie*" toasts with Żubrówka vodka, and *bigos* at midnight. I want to observe the old tradition of my husband and me getting our hands tied with a white scarf, and I want a *mazurka* dance that ends when we fall down from exhaustion.

This might never happen in my lifetime.

The Holy Father, on the other hand, will speak again. The vocal cords were very close to the incisions I made. I definitely thought about making a few fateful snips too many. He almost lost his voice for good.

I confess this to you, but there is nobody who can forgive me, especially not the patient.

He is not my Holy Father.

SEA SALT

She put me on a train, this crazy girl. And she was sitting in the seat beside me.

"I want you to know exactly why we're doing this," Dorota said, wiping the can opener clean on her sleeve.

"Because you want to see me naked again?"

"Yes, but that's beside the point. It's because freedom fighters can't be inhibited."

"I can whip it out now, if you like."

When I had told Doktor Dorota about my sex and nudity issues, she prescribed a trip to the Baltic Sea. I wasn't sure about the exact details, though I knew we were going to get naked. A lot of old folks go there to dance panty-free in the freezing water for its healing properties, to cure eczema and rosacea with salt. Slough off their malaise with freshly dead sponge.

I just hoped her plans didn't include something idiotic like seeing the solo concert that David Gilmour was scheduled to play in the seaport city of Gdańsk: one guitarist does not a Pink Floyd reunion make. Besides, everyone knows that Roger Waters was the heart of Pink Floyd, or rather, the germ.

Dorota and I hollowed out our bread rolls and laced them with śledź from a tin, dripping with tomato sauce and lemon juice. A stink bomb, quite literally; eating marinated herring on a train is the international sign for "don't sit in our cabin." So is yanking shut the orange polyester blinds on the cabin door window. In a country as densely populated as Poland, you must protect leg-room to the death. We stretched our legs and ate, ate, ate, washing it down with *herbatka* from a thermos. This was our *pociąg pospieszny* to paradise.

The Polskie Koleje Państwowe (PKP) is a notoriously ancient institution that uses maps and timetables corresponding to towns no longer serviced and rail lines long buried in weeds. Trains are never late, because they always come unexpectedly. The irritable clerks are happy to remind you, as they throw your change through the slot under the bulletproof "customer service" window, that there is no alternative. The PKP would choose steam locomotives for their *pospieszna* express trains, given the choice, just to make you late.

For the first ten minutes of the trip, our only view of paradise was of the unmoving platform. I was anxious to get going and fetched the ticket-taker.

"*Proszę bardzo*, can you tell me when the train will depart?" I said. I hoped my earnestness would eventually trigger Dorota to say something snarky to him.

The ticket-taker spoke into a radio and listened, nodding his head and saying "*no.*" No means yes in Polish.

"There are some cows. They refuse to move and we cannot find the farmer."

I looked to Dorota for help, but she was too busy playing tic-tac-toe on her arm to escalate the situation. I guess there were some battles she didn't feel like fighting, and that was just fine.

We finally got moving, and left Kraków for the seven-hour trip north. We passed a string of villages, towns, and cities that may or may not have been on the map.

Kielce (quaint)

Skarżysko-Kamienna (boring)

Radom (medieval)

Warszawa (overrated, yet still the international face of the country)

Ciechanów (where we saw the offending cows shot and splayed on the embankment)

Malbork (castles, ghosts, and tourists)

Trains make me want to smoke, but we had no cigarettes. As the train ripped through the countryside, we stood in the corridor and hung our arms out the window, letting the foliage whip our skin and stain it with chlorophyll. In Poland, trees are not trimmed unless they're in someone's yard. Weeds are not weeds; they're wild plants that elder townsfolk search for and lure into garbage bags. I wish I were old.

We were invaded in Tczew: a platoon of soldiers boarded the train. It could've been straight out of a World War II movie, but their rifles looked like they were in such bad condition that I doubt they worked. Our car became a virtual barracks, with a kennel of twenty-year-old boys drinking Okocim beer from cans—the cheap stuff, let me tell you—and flirting with Dorota when she passed in the corridor. We shut ourselves in our cabin until we got to Gdańsk.

Still, they could've gang-banged Dorota any time they wanted. It would start with a polite knock on the door, and then it would be unstoppable rape, blood, laughter, and buckets of semen.

Was she going to fuck me on the beach?

When we got to Gdańsk, Dorota steered us away from the *Solidarność* monuments, not wanting any distractions to derail our afternoon of fun and discovery. She knew, the smart biscuit, that if I saw the wall at the shipyards that unemployed electrician Lech Wałęsa first stood on to stir brio in the workers, I'd never want to leave. The cradle of the Solidarity Movement was a warm place for babies of any age.

The tram to the beach took forty-five minutes. The sun was already starting to wane, and we had run out of food, but the sight of white sand and blue water quelled our appetites and made us happy again. Dorota stripped two hundred metres from shore and bolted for the sea. Nobody wears clothes at the wet lip of the Baltic, especially not the sick. We all need some kind of healing.

I stripped, too.

The city does not feel like this. There is no salty mist coating your body like you're a potato chip. Your scrotum does not shrivel, and your nipples don't swell in the cool wind. You do not walk through clusters of people without seeing them, without assuming they are sand-dune formations.

We swam together for a while, in opposite directions, until we couldn't see each other anymore. I lost Dorota's head in the sun's reflection; I mistook her for a whitecap several times.

I swam to where she was floating, and together we stared at the beach, just one of the horizons to look at.

"Why do you suppose you're so interested in fire?" she asked.

"I like you a lot," I said, "but I don't like your question. It's slanted. You're asking me for a hypothesis, but you know full well I have a real answer."

"Please, let's not fight out here."

"Then where?"

We weren't far from Westerplatte, where the Nazis had first invaded Poland to kick off the war, turning what was then called the Free City of Danzig and subsequently, the rest of Europe, into Silly

Putty. I mentioned this fact to her.

"You think too much," she said, then dipped her head momentarily under the waterline. "And you don't make it easy to be your friend."

"Sorry ... I'm being stupid," I said. "Nobody has ever asked me before, that's all. They just think I'm trying to get attention or that I'm a psycho, but they really have no idea." The water was loosening me up, massaging me as it would wash undulations into a sand bar. "It started when I was a kid. There was a huge fire the colour of crayons. Yellow, red, orange. Red-orange. It turned a house into a volcano and it scared the shit out of me."

She was stretched out on the surface of the sea, as flat as a stingray. Her lips were blue. I felt numb.

"Whose fire was it?"

I bit my tongue. Fire belongs to everyone. That's why I could hold Chicago to my chest; I would never have been able to burn something that wasn't mine. Still, I knew what she meant. I would tell her someday, but I didn't want to think about death and melting toys and death and frantic neighbours and death and screams and having to start a new school, not there where I was pleasantly discovering conch shells by shuffling my feet.

"A little boy's," I said, and we left it at that.

There must be a word for this: speaking of fire in the middle of the sea. What is it?

"Time to go," Dorota said. "We might burn out here, and besides, the online messageboard said that the action starts around dinner-time."

We bought some corn-on-the-cob from a friendly older couple, slathered it with *smalec* (you don't want to know) and chomped down through the fat as Dorota led us west, to an isolated part of the beach.

I had gotten dressed after drying off, though I was surprised that Dorota let me. She was walking with lead feet, kicking up buckets of sand. Amber hunting? Quite possibly. She had nice tits and a wonderful thatch of wayward pubic hair. Rebel child, from the toes up.

We passed a *szopka* made of driftwood. It was a mini log cabin protecting carvings of Mary, Joseph, and Baby Jesus from the elements. The Three Magi were hanging out in the sand behind the cradle, working out my fate.

Then I saw a penis. Then two. Big suckers, too. Men were playing hide-and-go-seek with each other, fucking and sucking on blankets hidden in the bluffs and behind tufts of reeds.

Dorota's toe found a used condom, lubed and sand-speckled. "We're here," she said, and led us deeper into the bluffs.

We found two men giving each other head, an awkward 69 on tiny tea towels. They were naked except for two yellow sports watches, the giant waterproof ones with chronometers. They jumped when they saw us, likely because they didn't expect to see a naked chick.

"Please continue," Dorota said. "We just want to watch because Radeki here has never done this."

We sat down beside the men in the sand and ogled them from close up. The sounds were getting me hot, the ones they drown out in porn videos: when you're sucking, you pull your mouth away a millimetre too far, and your lips flap in the sudden vacuum ... or the uncensored fart, harmless and human.

They came here, I realized, for the same reason I hid in the Sportowe boiler room: to get on (get off?). The trouble is that neighbours, strangers, and family are always on the lookout for faggot activity. You live in perpetual fear of a crowbar smashing your skull and of death coming before you can feel the cum run out from your lips.

You want to experience every sensation, especially if it's your last.

Dorota stuck her hand down my pants and held my nuts, weighed them. A seagull screamed over us. I laughed because their shadows were much warmer than the ones cast by the crows of Kraków.

She undressed me, and I fumbled to keep up. It was more motherly than sexual, and I basked in the comfort her touch brought me. She laid me down in the sand and buried me one scoop at a time with her little dumptruck hands. She stopped to inspect my foreskin, thumbing it from the inside as if cleaning the rim of a glass. I didn't think, I felt; I felt like a sea creature, perhaps a coral or an urchin.

I guess she judged me sensitive enough to warrant protection, because she wrapped my cock in a gingham handkerchief before continuing the burial work. Soon only my face was exposed. By showing me how to be naked under the safety of sand, Dorota gave me freedom, and there's no way you can repay someone for that.

Our men spasmed, I could see, and their leg muscles hardened to steel. They emptied cum into each other's mouths and when they spat, they spat sand, and nothing else. Filtering each other impeccably.

"I'm Michał," one of them introduced himself, wiping his lips.

"Can you two uncover Radeki?" Dorota said.

"Is he a gay?" Michał asked. Just looking at his facial scruff gave me perineum tingles. He was a curious fellow, and he poked at my sarcophagus. I festered in my pile of sand, I tell you, and it was absolutely cudowny.

"When you get to the bottom, you'll find that he is many things," Dorota told him. "My one request, in exchange for giving you this honour, is that you denude him a few grains at a time, but no quicker." She turned to me and petted my chin. "It's much slower than taking off your clothes, darling."

And then she was gone, a metre away from me, hopelessly lost in a book. She sucked on her hair and I could smell the sweetness of it. It looked like strands of licorice, but probably tasted like lavender conditioner.

The waves got louder as the sun settled into a comfortable orange. These sadists took their time. Michał asked me question after question, fascinated by my tales of "the South" (he had never been to Kraków). I found out that they were boyfriends, and that they both lived with their parents.

I felt Michał scratch on my gingham dick sack. My skin emerged slowly, dusty with salt and utterly at their mercy, for my limbs had fallen asleep beyond the point of needles and tacks (needles and pins?). I was rock hard.

Michał gestured at the throbbing handkerchief.

"Excuse me, madam, perhaps this belongs to you?"

Dorota held out her hand. The boys ripped it off me and gave it to her. She then returned to her reading, which I found ridiculously sexy. A book lures you into a state of bodily comfort and then, once your limbs are placed just right, finger-fucks your insides. I wanted to be the book, stretching her open a little wider with every pithy sentence.

I didn't feel shame, nor did I hear any priestly voices reciting scripture. I wondered if this was a trick, if I was being saved by mere distraction. Did it matter? Instead of shame, I felt Michał's tongue trace figure-eights on my belly until it generated more electricity than I could bear. I wanted him to knife my gut open and drink its contents—semen would flow too slowly from my dick.

Then my own legs turned to steel and I thought of the shipyards, the workers pouring decades of anguish into perfectly constructed hull girders.

Dorota looked up from her book, turned to me, and said nonchalantly, "The voice of passion is better than the voice of reason. The passionless cannot change history."

She kissed me on the lips, and I came. It was an epic shudderfuck.

She stared at the pool of goo on my stomach, and I wondered if she had been watching me the whole time, waiting for it.

"Miłosz?" I said.

She nodded.

Then Dorota taught me that orgasm is not the end. She made me burn two pages of the Bible and scatter the ashes in the water. I didn't even have to read them to know what they said:

> If a man lies with a man as one lies with a woman, both
> of them have done what is detestable. They must be put to
> death; their blood will be on their own heads.
> —Leviticus 20:13

> In the same way the men also abandoned natural rela-
> tions with women and were inflamed with lust for one
> another. Men committed indecent acts with other men,
> and received on themselves the due penalty for their
> perversion.
> —Romans 1:27

I forgot the sound of the apostle Paul's voice that very day, but now I hear Czesław Miłosz every time I cum.

YOUTUBE

The stadium lights cast four shadows for every player on the nuclear-green pitch. Nobody, however, is watching the match.

Zoom in on a guy in a blue tracksuit climbing a steel fence and unfurling a flag. Someone on the other side throws a bottle at his head and he falls. The Holy War has begun. This is Wisła Kraków versus Cracovia. The city is riven in two because good fans don't mix. When there are two home teams, nobody wants to be the "visitor."

Someone is bound to get hurt.

The match has barely begun, and the announcer is already hoarse.

A Wisła striker feints a pass.

Cracovia wastes a slide tackle on nothing but air.

The goalkeeper gets hit in the head with a plastic cup. He flips the bird, but doesn't know where to aim his middle finger because he can't find his assailant. The camera pans to the nearest grandstand, which is quite far away. There must have been a rock taped to the inside of the cup for it to travel such a distance.

Cracovia takes possession. The grandstand is composed of two trenches separated by a chain-link fence three metres high: a tangle of barbed wire, coach effigies with noose necklaces, and scraps of torn clothing. We hear two chants crashing together into cacophony, laced with obscenities. This ritualized hatred is what keeps the city together. Nobody hears the whistle.

The referee calls an obstruction on Wisła.

He flashes a yellow card to the offending player and awards Cracovia an indirect free kick. Pan to the crowd cheering and booing him in equal measure. This Holy War has been rehearsed for exactly 100 years, and everyone knows what part they play.

The Cracovia striker spits for luck on the penalty mark, kisses his fingers, and touches them to his cleats. His hair is wet, likely with beer.

A banana kick takes everyone by surprise.

A midfielder leaps to make a header.

The ball misses the net and soars into the stands. The player's head must be warped.

Kto wygra mecz? Wisła, Wisła

Kto wygra mecz? Wisła, Wisła

The fans do not demand technical excellence. They demand a goal, even if it means they have to snipe the goaltender, threaten the referee with cash and bribe him with death, or jump on the field to take care of business themselves.

The real action is in the stands, not on the pitch.

The TV station hasn't properly adjusted its cameras for the blaze of fireworks that suddenly lights up the crowd. An electric, tangerine flash obscures the stadium. The picture comes back into focus on a sky filled with billowing red smoke. The camera zooms in on two men, ecstatic, with burns on forearms that they hold out proudly. Pyrotechnics char tracksuits like sheets of looseleaf. Faces, no matter how animated, do not reveal the divide between pain and defiance.

This video will be played to grandchildren. "I'm the one shaking my fist in the air. See?" Everyone wants history to catalogue them as the agitator that stung like horseradish in the nose. The players have it easy because they don't have to fight.

Kto wygra mecz? Cracovia, Cracovia

Kto wygra mecz? Cracovia, Cracovia

The Pet Shop Boys get royalties from the Holy War, because most of the chants are set to the melody of their hit "Go West."

A throw-in from the sidelines, and it lands among dangerous feet. What appears to be a Wisła defender gets a taste for blood and runs afield, running way past his assigned territory. He's wearing leather gloves.

He fakes out an opponent with sleight of foot and meets himself on the other side of the centre line. Makes it to the penalty arc and passes to a teammate. The ball bounds right back to him. This has turned into a personal mission.

The crowd is now finally watching the match. They tumble over bleacher seats trying to get closer.

We see that the Wisła defender is actually the Wisła goalkeeper, come to make his nemesis piss his shorts. One net is empty and the other is nervous. The score is nil-nil.

The announcer screams that never has a Polish goalie scored a goal. He would make history. The crowd unites for a few seconds, cheering the goalie. Hatred melts in a common hope.

Poles are addicted to history.

But then a rear defender makes an illegal charge, the attacking goalie does a somersault and loses the ball, and the game ends in a tie. History is denied a photo-finish. Six riot vans storm the field and prepare to blast the crowd with water cannons. But tonight, they don't need to; the fans are strangely peaceful, and they leave the stands chanting:

Polska biało-czerwoni!

Polska biało-czerwoni!

The Village People make a few bucks from this version of "YMCA."

There are only sporadic fistfights as the fans stream out together. They do not tear the metal fence down and attack each other with blunt objects, as they normally do. The announcer says that this is an omen for trouble to come. Football matches are allowed to end nil-nil, according to the rules, but not the Holy War. Somebody has to lose.

Sharp cut to a deserted part of town.

Twenty men walk with purpose, swinging their arms as if carrying baseball bats. Their hands are empty. This is overtime, citizen-style. A camera operator is smart to follow them.

The microphone picks up bits of their conversation:

"We can't be far from the faggot club. This is the corner where they catch taxis, always in twos."

"Sometimes in threes. When [muffled] the third one has to go on top."

"They will go to hell holding hands. We will send them there quicker."

(Interlocutor speaks unclearly.)

"No, Cracovia takes it up the ass. That's why they run slowly, because all the [muffled] is pouring out of them."

"*Kurva*, you are making me horny to beat up a queer."

"Just go home with them in the taxi. Say that you have a foreskin, and they will fight over you. My brother [muffled]. The hospital wouldn't take them because [muffled]."

The hooligans walk through a parking lot to a red-brick industrial building, and then climb a metal stairway. The gay club doesn't have a sign—there is never a sign—but someone has spraypainted four words that identify it quickly:

SOLIDARITY FOR POLISH QUEERS

We hear the thump of 1990s house. The men are about to tramp in and destroy human bodies, but then they freeze and turn around. They have discovered their shadow and look right into the camera. We suddenly see sideways footage of the city skyline. The sound is still running.

"*Kurrrva*. It's a faggot."

The camera operator has caught them visiting a gay nightclub.

"Do you want to die, motherfucker?"

Scuffling sounds. Shoes squeak.

"Let's rape him."

"The scissor kick. Wisła would have won if they did the scissor kick. Let's show him how we score a goal. Now your face will become a football, motherfucker."

"[Muffled] been born."

DEAR MAGPIE

May I call you that? I think the name suits you, not only for your crazy appetite, but also for the colouring of your hair. Hope you don't find it too weird.

After some reflection, I realize I was being weak when I refused to answer your question fully while we were floating in the Baltic Sea. You know, the question about my interest in fire. I didn't think I was ready, but you've since shown me that jumping head-first into something is the best strategy.

Here it goes.

When I was a little *dziecko* of six years old, my favourite toy was a green plastic *smok*. Dragon toys were hard to come by (this was before Communism ended), so I was lucky to have an American model with such exciting advanced features as movable jaws and interlocking scales. By itself, the toy would have been lifeless, but my favourite book—*The Legend of the Smok Wawelski*—gave it blood and teeth.

The *smok* and I had a love affair. I remember waking up in the middle of the night to play with him under the covers when my *matka* and *papa* had gone to sleep. I illuminated his cave—a tent under the sheets—with a tiny flashlight, and fed him his midnight snack of cookie crumbs. He always did as he was told, unlike his literary alter ego.

One time, my *matka* caught us awake. She turned on my bedroom light, and the smok instantly fell asleep.

"Radeki, lights out means lights out. A growing boy needs to rest."

"I'm not growing anymore, I promise. I haven't grown in a week. I even measured against the door to make sure."

"My silly smok, you will grow for a long time."

I loved it when she told me that. I was disappointed that my little green friend would never grow. Forever confined to the skeleton of a dwarf. *Jaka szkoda.* (Which means *quelle horreur.*)

"Anyway, I don't want you playing with this flashlight," she continued. "It has given your father some trouble in the past."

The flashlight was not American like my best toys were. It was Soviet-issue, and it fizzled reliably. One time, the batteries leaked corrosive acid all over the inside, and we had to clean it out with baking soda and vinegar. In those days, it was hard to get new equipment unless you were well-connected. Either my *papa* didn't know anyone important, or he was banking up his favours for something big. *Matka* and I were recycling long before it became an official program, because we had no choice.

"The smok and I will make it our royal duty not to give trouble. We will eat in the dark."

She reached under my pillow and removed two shortbread *muszelki.*

"No, you will eat at the table, and you will sleep in the dark. Tell your dragon that tomorrow is a very busy day. We are driving to Zakopane for an excursion with Brother Father. You know how he loves the snow."

"I don't have to tell him," I said. "Smok's ears are very good. He heard you."

Brother Father was not my *papa*, but a priest who had been living with us for several years. He was a boarder who paid his lodging faithfully, and who helped us out with our spiritual troubles, as pedestrian as they were. We were a good Christian family, save for a few forgivable habits like drinking alcohol on Sunday (*Matka*), smoking on the toilet (*Papa*), and listening to the Beatles (*Matka* and *Papa*). Brother Father corrected us mildly and brought us closer to God, powered by my mother's cooking and by coffee she fortified secretly with shots of cognac.

You might say this arrangement had the blessing of the church and was part of the *Out-of-the-Pew-and-into-the-Home* program, enforced mercilessly by the Communists. In other words, Brother Father had no church to go to, and we were his only parishioners.

"It's not a secret," my mother would tell me. "Just tell people he's your uncle, and that he's too sick to work."

I wasn't allowed to know his name, just in case I squawked. We called him Brother Father and nobody slipped up, not even once.

Or so I thought.

One night after lights out, *smok* and I were playing in his den without detection. The flashlight was giving off sparks and I was thrilled: fire breath in a convenient tube. With a simple fluke, I had vaulted twenty years ahead of the toy industry. *Park Jurajski*, eat my underpants.

But I'll never understand why she let me keep the flashlight. I wish she had taken it away, and if I'd rebelled, I would've wanted her to lash me with a belt and flense my skin into strips. But no, she let me keep the damn thing.

I read from *The Legend of the Smok Wawelski* in a loud whisper, hoping to increase the heartbeat of my toy dragon to a rhythm approximating my own.

Magpie, I'll try to retell the story as I remember it, but I'm warning you, my memory for literature sucks compared to yours. And you've probably already noticed that I get everything mixed up when telling stories (including places and dates).

I have, however, corrected spelling mistakes that I remember from the original book (the Russians never cared to learn Polish very well).

Chapter 1

Once upon a time, there lived a King in the Royal Castle on Wawel Hill. He ate piggishly and fucked fair maidens from near and far, orchestrating abortions in the dungeon when they got pregnant. What king would want a shoal of jealous sons lining up to poison him and steal the throne?

One day, terrible news rocked the city: someone had found a huge fire-breathing dragon nesting in a cave beneath the castle. Sheep, cattle, and chickens started to disappear, and the cityfolk realized that the Smok must be eating them to satisfy his voracious appetite, belching eyelashes and effluvium after every snack.

(Dorotka, I've drawn you a picture of the Smok Wawelski below, in colours with much better fidelity than in my Soviet-issue book. They made him brown. LOL.)

[Picture of a dragon in crayon. His body is an equilateral triangle, shaded emerald green and covered with striated tiles supposed to be scales. Rudimentary legs jut out. He has a Pac-Man mouth with yellow studs for teeth, and he's exhaling blue smoke by the cheek-load.]

The pigs and boars and *kozy* were not enough to keep the Smok Wawelski happy. They were possibly not nutritious enough, or maybe too noisy, so the Smok—to the great horror of Kraków—began to target young virgin girls for breakfast. How do we know they were virgins? The fathers who lost their daughters gave detailed descriptions, while making the sign of the cross, of the intact hymens of their offspring: crescent-shaped bands from the two to eleven o'clock positions, no tissue at six o'clock, fimbriated perforations in the shape of praying hands. Whatever they said, it was convincing enough to nail down the Smok's exact breakfast habits, and the King ordered little girls across the land to stay in their homes. And yet, the dragon always managed to get one, to suck the flesh from her bones, and to leave the skeleton in a neat, crumpled pile at the entrance to his den.

Unfortunately, presumed masculinity in monsters is a hallmark of children's literature. In future retellings, and at your request, I will jam the signal with a more bent monster. (A girl, possibly.)

My book lit up when I got to the end of the chapter; the sparks from the flashlight had jumped onto the paper and turned to embers. The embers grew into flame, and the page I was reading blackened, curled, and floated away. A sheet of ash; spent words.

This, Dorota, is when it all began. Sorry it has taken me so long to tell you.

I dropped the book and ran to the foyer. I zipped up my winter jacket, threw on my boots and mittens, and ran outside. We were one of the unlucky families with a bungalow. You can only fit so many people into apartment blocks, we were told, so some had to live separately—medievally—without the conveniences of modern life. I suspected that our living situation had something to do with Brother Father (I wish I knew his name), even though we never told a soul about him.

I ran outside to the street and just stared at the house. The darkness was total. One of my mittens was on the wrong hand; my thumb wriggled without finding its sheath. The snow was deep, and it crept into my boots. I was waiting for my parents to run out in their winter clothes to comfort me, to rescue me from the fire I had already escaped.

What kid ever thinks their parents need help? You're trained since infancy to believe that they hold the keys to medicine, education, law, opening jars, gardening, ripping off bandages, starting cars, and finding money. They are wizards with fire, and forbid you to know its secrets.

Certainly, I didn't need to save them from anything. Besides, I was too little to fight a real dragon.

I knew something was wrong when they still weren't outside after a few minutes, when the living room drapes exploded orange and melted into goops (I now know they were synthetic polymer). I peed my pants, sure that the Smok Wawelski had come to life and was going to eat my parents and Brother Father. I heard the dragon knock down the curtain rod with his arched back, and then smash the glass ornaments on our Christmas tree. Crushing my present, for sure.

Still, nobody came out, and I wondered if they were already dead. Icy armour crept over my leg; urine freezes quickly.

Then, my parents' bedroom window flew open, and dear *Papa* fell naked through the blinds and into the bushes by the house. This was not the hero I was expecting. Thick grey smoke followed him and continued upward into the night.

Papa ran barefoot across the snow-covered yard, cussing and scream-ing my name. His ass was bloody where the frozen bush-twigs had lacerated it. I could tell by the notes in his voice that he wasn't angry. He was scared, like I was. I didn't say anything, and he ran back into the house through the front door. Smoke pushed him out, so he got down on all fours and crawled inside. I wondered if the last I would see of my father would be his pendulous, hairy balls.

"Please save *Matka* and Brother Father," I said, after he had disap-peared inside. "*Matka* first. Don't save me. I'm already outside."

Dear Dorota, it is incredible how one can collect a lifetime of "why"s in the span of a few minutes. Maybe we're born with a mech-anism to create these questions, so that we can answer them later in life and have something meaningful to do. What do you think?

Now the house glowed cherry from all the windows, and I could hear the crackle of the dragon munching everything I loved. Pulverizing the family flashlight in his back molars, I was sure. He shattered glass in his teeth, and bashed holes in the roof with his thorny head. The whole house soon puffed smoke, puffed madness, funnelling into a monstrous pillar that twisted ugly into the night, its blackness sucking up shards of flame. Poland didn't have tornadoes, I knew, but the Bible promised many impossible things:

> And the Lord went before them by day in a pillar of cloud
> to lead them along the way, and by night in a pillar of fire
> to give them light, that they might travel by day and by
> night.
> —Exodus 13:21

Was this the salvation that Brother Father was supposed to bring us?

The heat had melted my frozen pee, and I remember thinking that I had nowhere to change. As if it mattered. I ripped off my jacket because the fire was heating the zipper like a branding iron. I burned my chin more than once.

Papa screaming my *matka*'s name

The fire truck screaming my house's name

Me screaming my *papa*'s name

The neighbour screaming the name of God

The firefighter's radio screaming that the water was shut off

God screaming the name of the beast

The Smok Wawelski screaming the name of its next, and possibly last, meal

Brother Father screaming my name

The meal screaming not to be eaten, *The fire is too hot, too hot, why won't anyone save me, my nightgown is burning, now my skin now my hair, so hot, God I have always believed in you, let me hold my son one last time, do not let him see me like this, kurvakurvakurva, is there a sin I don't know about, tell him*—

I couldn't hear the rest, no matter how close I got to the bedroom window.

I was deaf to the most important words ever spoken to me.

"Tell him."

Brother Father and *Papa* came running out of the house and hugged me, telling me not to listen, blocking my ears. Telling me not to worry, that it was just a hysterical neighbour. I still hadn't moved. The world had changed, and I hadn't moved a centimetre. Since when were things allowed to change without you? How was that fair?

Later, a *detektyw policji* asked me the strangest questions, and I tried my best to answer them.

"Do you remember how the fire started?"

She wouldn't understand a thing about the Smok Wawelski, so there was no point in telling her the truth.

"In the Christmas tree."

"Then you ran outside."

"Yes."

"Why were you dressed in your winter clothes?"

"Because it was cold outside."

"So you had time to get dressed, but not to warn your parents?"

I fiddled with one of the buttons on my pajamas. She didn't know how it was. She couldn't know. She held a tissue to my nose, told me to blow, and pressed on with her inquiry.

"Radek, why didn't you answer your father when he called your name?"

"Because I didn't want him to think I was talking from inside the house," I said.

"Why would he think that? You were behind him."

"I don't know. *Papa* doesn't like it when I pee my pants. I was waiting for them to dry."

"Your papa was naked."

She should've known, dear Dorota, that the "why" questions have no real answers, that we can only give fake ones to placate, and that some of us are better at lying than others. She should've known that I was dazed and terrified, and that my little body was battling shock and hypothermia. The bitch should've given me a blanket.

"Did your parents ever fight? It's okay to talk about it. Your *papa* said it was okay to talk about anything with me."

They didn't care about my *papa*. As I got older, I began to piece things together: why the firefighters had come late, why the water was "turned off" on our block. It must've been because my *papa* refused to be a stool pigeon for the Communist Party, and they probably knew about Brother Father, too.

"Do you remember anything else about the fire?"

What a fucking question.

I refused to give any more answers that she could twist maliciously and write on her clipboard.

Dorota, I hope you never have a housefire, if you haven't already. Because decades later, you will not remember how long you stood in the cold, or how many fire trucks there were, or when you realized your mother had become a charred skeleton, or the last words she ever cried to you through a throat that was blistering and peeling away. You will not recall the changing colour of the flames, but you will make them up. You will reinvent everything.

The smell of smoke, on the other hand, will never leave you.

You'll be lying in bed about to go to sleep, and charcoal will suddenly fill your nose. You'll sprint through the house, taking inventory of your combustibles and sniffing cracks in the wall, but it'll only be a phantom scent. Furniture will smell like campfire, and the sulphur in your shit will make you jump off the toilet seat. This will happen repeatedly, but there will never be a pillar of smoke to guide you. Perpetually lost, I'm afraid.

Magpie (is "girlfriend" better?), I'll have to transcribe the remaining chapters of The Legend of the Smok Wawelski some other time.

I'm getting sleepy.

Love,

Radeki

KRYPTOZOOLOGY

"Poland is clearly in Eastern Europe," I told Dorota as we walked through the main gates of the Poznań Zoo.

"It *used* to be Eastern when it was Eastern Bloc," she said. "But the map was redrawn after free elections. By 1990, we had become Central."

"Central is nowhere," I said, buying us two tickets. I noticed that my wallet was dangerously empty; I was going to have to destroy another city soon to pay the rent.

"And Eastern is somewhere?"

"It's extreme."

Our train excursion to Poznań had been fun because we'd found a thrilling new way to claim a cabin to ourselves: taking off our shoes and hanging our funky socks on the curtain rod.

"Let's find the Elephant House," she said.

We had come to see, with our own eyes, what *Rzeczpospolita* had once described as "the wild beast of the Book of Revelation." Elephants weren't very biblical animals, but evil apparently took many forms. It appeared that Ninio was gaga over the other male elephants, and wouldn't "mingle" with the resident female, even when the keepers—it was rumoured—sprayed her pussy with peanut extract. He had to be an envoy of Satan.

Poznań city counsellor Michał Grześ of the right-wing Law and

Justice Party was beside himself. And he was beside a UK *Daily Mail* journalist when he said, "We didn't pay thirty-seven million złotych for the largest elephant house in Europe to have a gay elephant."

Only they did.

Grześ hadn't planned on building a shrine to the biological basis for same-sex attraction, but that's how it turned out. And they could spray all the peanut extract in the world, but Ninio would still be a fag.

I planned to whisper into Ninio's ear never to lumber away from a 93.3 millilitre ejaculation of semen. That the fastest way to male pachyderm orgasm was a prostate massage through the anus.

The macaws tore a complaint as we passed them. A wake of buzzards were gnawing on a pile of rat carcasses.

Aside from Ninio, I was excited to visit the namesakes of the songs on Pink Floyd's *Animals* album. Unquestionably, 1977 was a good year for disobedient "Sheep," "Dogs," and "Pigs on the Wing." Yes, these are farm animals, but far from ordinary. I couldn't wait to point out their quirks to Dorota.

A float of crocodiles chattered their teeth. Capybaras brayed. Really? I probably had the sounds mixed up.

When I was a kid, my wind-up Animal See N Say went wonky all the time. The recorded animal sounds rarely matched the pictures. "The pig says 'moo.' The dog says 'ribbit.'" I pulled that cord thousands of times and learned again and again that life in the animal kingdom was a fluid affair.

We continued walking through the menagerie of tourists and found the sheep pen. I was lucky the zoo was proud to showcase barnyard specimens because we caught the woolly bastards in full rut. The rams were tearing each other into pieces of souvlaki, fighting over the right to mate.

"Dorotka, look. They're wearing marking harnesses so they can draw on their fucks with a crayon. The keepers have to know who did who."

"How stupid and territorial," she said.

"Think of it as art."

Granny Smith Apple green means, "You're my slut-hole." Wild Blue Yonder means, "I like looking at the sky when we fuck," and Razzle Dazzle Rose is, "Love you, too."

A gulp of cormorants flew overhead, shitting on strollers and stealing ice cream sandwiches. The małpy were picking wszy out of each other's fur. Baboons flashed Crayola ass shows of Hot Magenta and Cerulean.

The sheep says "meow."

There were no dogs not posing as timberwolves.

We passed the pigs. I was about to explain to Dorota that a pig tongue has triple the taste buds a human's does, and that if a pig were to fly, other pigs wouldn't be able to see it. Swine, the darlings, are incapable of looking up. But I kept quiet, unsure if she believed even half of what I told her.

"Where would Ninio go if he escaped?" she asked.

"He'd probably wander southeast to Moldova, and then the Ukraine forest. Fossils show that the Tiraspol species comes from the area."

"How do you know all this?"

"That's what the tabloids say. They propose that the zoo kick him out."

"What if we break him out?" she said. "You have a lot of experience with fire."

"You want to see me in jail, don't you?"

"No, but we have to take action before someone poisons him."

It thrilled me that she was getting infected with my love for fire. I ached to know exactly how much, but you can't just ask someone that question flat-out.

"Are you proposing a controlled blaze?" I said.

"Don't be gutless. We're not here to do half-assed work." She dangled her complicity in front of me like a piece of *gorzkiej czekolady*.

"As long as we don't kill any animals. Let's survey the area first, then discuss the details."

"Unless you're going to scope your way out of a rescue mission."

"Sweet Dorota, I'm not afraid of fire, and if you want me to prove it to you, I'll light your hair like a fuse, right here, right now."

"You're cute," she said.

Geese gabbed and a mob of emus painted the fence with urine.

"Does Ninio live in a spaceship?" she asked, pointing straight ahead.

There it was. The Elephant House, swooping arches forming a three-storey dome, a pine and glass hill rising out of the earth. It was as opulent as a brand-new football stadium and as combustible as a helium balloon.

Grześ had whined in the *Rzeczpospolita*, "We were supposed to have a herd, but as Ninio prefers male friends over females, how will he produce offspring?"

He was being polite, of course. What he really meant, was, "Spending thirty-seven million *złotych* was supposed to guarantee the future of the species, not provide panoramic viewing for a depraved theatre of anal sex."

Yes, the Elephant House was now sheltering the enemy.

It was crazy nice. There was a lake, a waterfall, and even a fake African village with restaurants and coffee shops made of thatched huts. The apex of the dome had a nave and transept, which made it look like a distended version of St Mary's Basilica.

Hypothetically speaking, it would burn quite evenly.

Ninio was built like a war elephant, with sun-weathered skin impervious to a variety of spears and harpoons. Throughout the history of battle, punks like him were sent ahead of the troops to trample mercilessly through the lines of the "other," wielding unbreakable tusks to gore and disembowel with, lodged in 7,000 kilos of unmovable meat.

It could be a personals ad, if it weren't so intimidating.

In case you haven't noticed, I spend hours reading up on all kinds of shit.

Dorota dangled her milky hand through the bars of the viewing gallery. It looked like a white candy cane with all the red sucked off, save for the pomegranate she was holding.

Ninio saw it and trundled over. It was a combo too delicious for a warrior to resist. Dorota's arm was as bad as gone.

In the Battle of Gaugamela, Alexander the Great sent a phalanx of fifteen war elephants ahead of him and his army. The Persian troops trembled so beautifully that Alexander later made a special sacrifice to the god of fear during his victory dinner.

Dorota took a bite of the apple and let the juice trickle down her finger.

Ninio broke into a gait.

Jazzberry Jam means, "Stamping you to death will be hot as fuck."

In a country where the biggest anti-gay argument—parroted by the masses—is that "homosexuality doesn't occur in nature," Ninio is the equivalent of an atom bomb. Gay activists wait day and night with handycams to catch him boffing other males, but the ground crew rigorously keeps them separated. That kind of footage is capable of destroying the country's moral foundation, whatever that means.

Dentition is spectacular: twenty-four molars out of twenty-eight teeth, replaced five times over a lifespan. Will grind your bones into a fine dust before swallowing.

Ninio reached us, plopped down on his big behind, and sniffed Dorota's hand with a curious trunk, brushing her wrists with bristly hairs. He grappled the pomegranate gingerly and let go, tried it again, and backed off. Only at Dorota's coaxing did he finally take the fruit, and then he sat there playing with it like a ball.

Some soldier.

This kid was not going to eviscerate anyone, nor was he likely to cock-whip any of his buddies in the near future.

"What do you think?" she said.

"*Il est tellement mignon,*" I said. "It's a shame that pine burns so quickly, because it's going to give him such a fright."

PLATINUM

Dear girlfriend (that is, if you don't mind),

I am now writing to you from the *Smocza Jama*, the Dragon's Den under Wawel Hill. Sightseers keep asking me for assistance, and I suspect it's because of my overalls: they think I work here. Why can't I successfully co-opt this blue-collar fashion item? You have yet to see me launch a serious attack on dressing norms, that's why. I'll update you when I have news on this front.

Years of heavily perfumed tourists have flushed out the dank of ages, but I can still feel the mustiness crawl over my skin. The stalactites have been broken clean off the ceiling, yet I can sense where their pointy tips would be. Too much light. Philistines and their halogens.

There's no question: the *Smok Wawelski lived here*. Dorota, this is the only fairy tale I believe in, and I've collected scientific evidence to back it up.

The tour guide is yapping about the history of this cave, but as you can understand, I'm not listening. We subscribe to the alternate histories, which are far more fascinating (not to mention accurate).

Allow me to continue *The Legend of the Smok Wawelski*. I'm sorry if my retelling lacks imagination, but the Soviets were much better in that department.

Chapter 2

No longer was the great dragon satisfied with young
virgin girls slathered in apple butter. Through a series of
clandestine communications, he demanded to have the
Princess—the King's daughter—as his next meal. The
Smok threatened that if the King declined this wish, he
would burn Kraków down in a single exhalation of fire.

That day, the King sent prince after knight after hero to
kill the dragon, but they were either cremated, or the
dragon sent them back with the words ROYAL HYMEN,
PLEASE carved neatly into their chests with a claw. What
could the King do?

[Illustration of the Smocza Jama. This one is drawn in fine
HB pencil, not in crayon like the last image. At the edges,
the recesses of the cave are shaded with cross-hatching,
quadrants of lines that get closer and closer until they
blur into underworld black. In the middle, the Smok is
about to swallow the reader, with tonsils the size of pyzy
coming right at ya.]

Real-world update. I just licked the cave wall. It's definitely
limestone.

A thermal analysis performed at Kraków's Institute of Inorganic
Chemistry and Technology has revealed that limestone and platinum,
when found together, can fuse as a result of sulphation.

Kryptozoologists point out that dragons could've easily created fire
by grinding platinum in their back molars while belching methane.

Kaboom. It's not so far-fetched; cows flame-fart over cooking fires all the time.

It's the fire tetrahedron—which sustains all life on earth—manifested through the mouth (and sometimes ass) of beasts. Can this be a lie?

Lick that. (Not you, girlfriend, and not that.)

Someone just asked me for a flashlight, and I nearly strangled them. Of course, you don't believe me. We both know I wouldn't hurt a *lecieć*.

Chapter 3

Just when the King had lost all hope and was dressing his daughter for destruction, a ten-year-old boy named Dratewka appeared. He presented a *wizytówka* that read "Shoemaker and Amateur Dragon-Slayer, Esq." He promised the King that he would be able to kill the Smok and save the Princess. The desperate King decided to give the runt a try.

Dratewka, wizard with a needle and thread that he was, took the skin of a dead sheep and stuffed it with sulphur, curry, chillies, and peppercorns. He gave krypto-sheep a set of maple legs and propped it up in front of the *Smocza Jama*. (Dorota, I am now standing in the very spot where he placed it.)

The Smok was expecting the Princess, but couldn't resist this plump appetizer. He swallowed the sheep whole. Instantly, his belly rioted against such strong spice, and he was overtaken by thirst. The dragon ran to Kraków's Wisła

River and took huge gulps of water. Still, nothing would quell the burn, so he drank and drank until the river was empty. Finally, with the entire Wisła in him, his stomach popped like a balloon and he died instantly. The elated King gave the prepubescent Dratewka his daughter's hand in marriage.

Now, hold on. I'm a firm believer in the Legend, Dorota, but there's no way I'm buying that last bit. The water would've shot out of the Smok's ass, for sure.

I remain unconvinced of his death.

Faithfully yours,

Radeki

ŚMINGUS DYNGUS

TV Polska 2 jingle

11:55 am – Special Interest News Piece

"We're back, and now we join our Kraków correspondent Augustyna Dobrowolski, who reports on a bizarre Easter phenomenon in the Stare Miasto. Augustyna, can you tell us what's happening?"

"Thanks, Piotr. As our viewers well know, Easter Monday is a day for raincoats, but *not* because of the weather. To celebrate Prince Mieszko's baptism on this day in 966, men splash women with water across the country, and almost everyone gets in on the fun."

"A time-honoured tradition."

"Yes, Piotr, and according to the legend, women who are splashed will marry within the *year*. Some of them, as we know, go *looking* for modern-day Prince Charmings armed with water pistols."

"And some run *away* from them, ha, ha. Augustyna, what's different about Śmingus Dyngus this year?"

"Well, witnesses earlier told me about two individuals armed with super-soaker guns—I want our viewers to picture what are almost mini-cannons that can hold litres of water—and surprisingly, they're spraying the *men*."

"Do you have any details on the shooters?"

"Yes, one of them is a woman and the other, if you believe it, is a man *dressed* as a woman, in a blonde wig, dress, and high heels."

"Oh, that's not surprising, Augustyna, considering what is scheduled to take place in downtown Kraków next Sunday. Gay protestors are planning a *so-called* March of Tolerance, despite not having a permit to do so. Police are concerned that these agitators may incite violence."

"Piotr, I'm told that residents and shopkeepers in the area are *quite* concerned for their safety."

"Yes, indeed. Now, Augustyna, I understand there's a twist to this story of the cross-dressing *bandits*. Can you tell our viewers what this is?"

"It's such a bizarre story. We have reports that after squirting unsuspecting men with water, these Easter vigilantes have been *jumping* over objects, not running, but literally *leapfrogging* over anything that gets in their way."

"Yes, Augustyna, this is known as *parkour*, a vicious extreme sport born in the suburbs of France and now running rampant across Poland. By all accounts, these homosexuals are quite athletic, but parkour is evidently not made for high heels."

"Ha, ha. Have a happy Śmingus Dyngus, Piotr, but please stay inside. You wouldn't want to get wet."

"We'll see you all tomorrow night."

TV Polska 2 jingle

MUSTH

For the first time in my life, I was actually hoping to see the police.

Dorota and I were walking through the streets of Kraków on a day almost like any other, slurping from a shared *mięty czekoladowe* ice cream cone. But there were subtle differences: that day, the sun was blocked by a giant rainbow flag, and we were marching with a few hundred queers who were either half-naked or wearing extravagant costumes. Except for me in my navy overalls, it was Pantone overload. We were happy to give the March of Tolerance some legs, but angry not to see any cops there to protect us.

We marched behind a truck-sized banner that said NIE LEKAJCIE SIE. To get this made, we were told, the organizers had to commission a discreet printing service, one that had specialized in samizdat during Communist rule. (As you can see, they forgot the accents.)

We had no floats. This was, after all, an illegal parade. Lech Kaczyński, mayor of Warsaw and leader of the Law and Justice Party, had been the first to ban a Polish pride parade. When angry Warsaw homos demanded an audience with him, he said he "refused to meet with perverts." That's okay with me. I wouldn't want to meet with Lech, either, because I wouldn't be able to stop myself from play-wrestling him to the ground and writing my name on his forehead. I have no problem being called a "pervert," but if anyone's going to violate my right to assemble, I want them to know exactly who they're fucking with.

Unfortunately, Lech's institutionalized hatred caught on, and it was no container of cherries.

Conversation gradually broke off as we left Universytet Jagielloński and marched through the Stare Miasto. Chanting took over:

Nie lękajcie się

Nie lękajcie się

Kraków is a small town with ancient ideas. You can feel ridiculous shouting slogans to a garlic peddler sweeping the dust off her square of sidewalk, even though you know she's part of the problem. Not joining the parade, we're told, is her crime.

Nie lękajcie się

Nie lękajcie się

Do not be afraid

How edifying to hear this yelled in your ear by a queen wearing purple leotards and flapping a pair of chiffon bumblebee wings. We were an unstoppable force of human unicorns, fairies, and seahorses—as well as a disproportionate number of birds—screaming at old ladies. Really, though, we were behaving like elephants in musth, a condition in which they experience a sudden 6,000 percent surge in hormones.

As noon rolled by and folks left work and school for lunch, we attracted a thicker crowd of onlookers. Some appeared friendlier than others. Smirks were hard to read, unless they were accompanied by the following chants:

Pedały do gazu

Pedały do gazu

Zoologists cannot properly investigate the musth phenomenon, because even the most docile elephant, when in that supercharged state, may kill any human it sees.

Dorota and I spotted the first T-shirt about thirty minutes into the parade. A guerrilla team was throwing this latest fashion item to the marchers who begged most for them. The front had an icon of a pink elephant, and the back said BECAUSE GOD MADE ME THIS WAY. KRAKOW STAMPEDE 2005.

One size fits all.

There was more Ninio hysteria: hand-painted cardboard signs that said, "SUCK MY TRUNK," "I LIKE IT ROUGH," and "SCREW PEA-NUTS, GIVE ME COCK."

That was the day I fell out of love with slogans, when I realized that such short combinations of words were never meant to carry so much meaning. Polish verbs are resilient, but the nouns simply melt under the pressure.

"I'm not putting on the damn T-shirt," I said to Dorota, throwing the rest of our ice cream on the cobblestone street. It melted almost instantly and settled in the cracks. "This is not what Ninio is supposed to be about."

"You know, they'll try to make us put it on."

"We'll tell them we're both recovering from elbow surgery. Can't lift our arms higher than a 'fuck you.'"

Elephants in musth go nuts, it's thought, when their temporal ducts swell and exert immense pressure behind the eyes. Imagine the pain from an abscessed tooth, but instead behind the cornea, pushing in-sanity with every throb.

Pedały do gazu

I was livid that Ninio was becoming a *maskotka*, and that I was now marching for God. I had long refused to be part of any Divine Plan, and I didn't see the point in borrowing and redressing arguments the church had devised. Subversion is cowardly that way. Sure, Ninio could help the gay cause, but his silkscreened image could do little for transphobia. And it was anathema to atheists.

Why couldn't Ninio simply fuck other males because he wanted to? Why did he need permission from above?

We quickened our pace, and the bullhorns squawked louder than ever. Perhaps we were feeling the pressure of the crowd, who now easily outnumbered us five to one, and who were getting nastier with their comments.

Dołożymy wam to, co Hitler zrobił z Żydami

Tomek, an acquaintance I knew from the gallery scene, cut through the ranks to us.

"Well, if it isn't S. Mok Wawelski, the art star. What are you cooking up next?"

"I have ideas for London, but San Francisco has post-fire details that blow my mind," I said. "Listen, did you know this was going to turn into a Fags for Jesus parade?"

"Radek, don't isolate yourself. We're in a position to score some victories this year, but you have to understand that it's going to happen collectively." The bumblebee buzzed past us, disguised as an elephant, fluttering his wings in time to the wave of fists punching the air. "We'd be fools to think we can do it alone."

"By 'we,' do you mean me?"

"I know what you guys are up to," Tomek said, motioning to Dorota, "and there is concern that this is causing division in the community."

I hoped I had misunderstood his slant. He pulled me aside, away from Dorota.

"Your friend is straight," he continued. "Have you ever thought about how this makes some of us feel? And what do you think she's really after?"

At first, elephant keepers thought that musth was sexual. Then they found the killing grounds where elephants had separated rhinos from their limbs and turned whole crashes of them into goulash for vultures.

"Fuck off," I said to Tomek, to keep myself from hitting him. "I hope you'll be happy when we win the right to be as fascist as our oppressors."

The shock on his face was priceless.

I rejoined Dorota.

"What did he say?" she asked. "I think he has a crush on you."

"He's an idiot," I said.

"You know, I missed a class for this," she said, punching me in the arm. I usually liked it when she erased the physical boundaries between us, but in this case, her timing was wrong. "I guess our elephant rescue plan just tanked."

"We'll find something else. Don't worry."

Dorota punched me again, or so I thought, but it wasn't a fist. It was a half-full can of Okocim beer that someone had thrown. The crowd was pressing in, narrowing the street into a sliver, and forcing us to march single-file. Our lead banner was scrunched like an accordion, and some of the onlookers coated our path with gobs of smoker's phlegm. It began to feel like a march to the gallows.

Dołożymy wam to, co Hitler zrobił z Żydami

Dołożymy wam to, co Hitler zrobił z Żydami

We'll do to you what Hitler did to the Jews

I saw Tomek blotting his bloody temple with a rainbow flag. He was the first to get beaned by a rock. I felt sorry we had quarrelled. After all, we were fighting for the same freedoms, just in different ways.

A hooligan smashed a bottle high on a brick wall above us, and I was done, for the day, with sentiment. I helped Dorota pick the shards of glass out of her hair and throw them back. Senseless, yes, but we were trapped. Then came the sweet whiff of human shit, the stench of bowel movements gone wrong. The crowd was pelting us with paper bags loaded with excrement, sealed, no doubt, with the kiss of death. The unicorn got covered in diarrhea.

Musth, some say, is a myth, the biggest grift in the animal kingdom. The fact is that all animals have pissy moments and need to express their rage on the nearest available sack of organs and bones.

Our bodies told us that this was no time for parkour. We could've leapt over cars, vaulted fire hydrants, and taken to air on the hands of our enemies, but it would've made poor news footage.

Pedały do gazu

Pedały do gazu

Gas the queers

This slogan wasn't aimed at her, or course, but Dorota was the queerest girl around, and I knew she felt the hit.

She pelted it back. Dorota gathered every slimy piece of feces she could find—wiping it off marchers, herself—and slung it wildly at the crowd. She even jumped over heads to aim curveballs at the neo-Nazis on the fringe. Her enthusiasm caught on, and soon we were all elbow-deep in this stinking revolt, fighting for our centimetres of cobblestone—and winning them.

Then sirens, and the beautiful sounds of police beating their riot shields with batons. Rescue. Only they came right at us, hitting and kicking faggots and dykes and gender-nonconformists and the bisexual threat, pounding us into pockets of solidarity and then breaking us up until we were alone and defenceless. Pulling our hair and dragging us down the street. The police arrested Tomek and a number of others, but not before detaching their earlobes from their heads with savage rips.

To please the crowd. To make the show worth losing a lunch hour for.

We were forced to run away. I would describe the expert parkour moves we executed, but all things considered, it's just too shameful.

ZOOMIE AWARD FINALIST

Whoever shot this video a) knows their way around the Elephant House at the Poznań Zoo and b) knows the hottest camera angles for porn.

High-angle shot:

Ninio is lifting his trunk at another elephant across the play area. "I'm coming hither," the move says. He struts over and corners the object of his lust. Her name is Elvira, says a clip-art bubble.

Dutch tilt:

A shot overused in sci-fi flicks, underused in the skin trade. The camera simulates Ninio peering curiously into her pussy. Meaty, wrinkled labia protrude. Skin has superior texture in this flick, and the resolution catches all.

Establishing shot:

Looking at Ninio's tectonic head as if from inside Elvira's cunt. A curious image with an unequivocal message: come pound the sweet fuck out of me.

Whip pan:

The camera pivots breakneck to Ninio's cock. It's a four-foot brown stalk with a curlicue bend, and it's snapping into a frenzy. Pre-cum drips in goopy ropes, enough sperm to father six million pounds of baby elephants, says a text bubble.

Extreme close-up:

Elvira's eye, a drippy orb. Subtle camera movement catches, in her black-hole pupil, the reflection of Ninio mounting her from behind.

Zoosexual cinema is governed by a screwy set of laws; like many vices, it can be consumed but not sold. Only the best films merit black-market circulation. They must be unerringly artistic and have glints of pathos, or they will never ignite word-of-mouth.

Bird's-eye shot:

Is there a camera crew? If it's only one person running from shot to shot, then it's damn impressive. Ninio hugs Elvira's back with his front legs and she farts a massive gust of wind under the exertion. Nothing makes an elephant porn movie go viral like a five-second raunch clip, because nobody does raunch like elephants.

Low-angle shot:

Extremely dangerous shot, with risk of trampling. So, *so* worth it. Ninio's dick is the god of all phalluses, and it jerks around trying to find Elvira's snatch, slapping her enormous MILF butt and hot thighs. It finally docks into her, stretching a gape and forcing out a bubbly queef. You'd never catch a noise that subtle in the wild.

Moving Dutch tilt:

The following could be cut-in footage, because the lighting is slightly different. The average consumer, however, will never notice.

Disoriented pleasure. Elvira doesn't have to shake her head back and forth, because the camera does it for her. She trumpets her body joy in cascading echoes, and we see inside her luscious mouth. It's wet and cavernous, with harmlessly round teeth. Cardinal rule of pachy-porn: always hint at a blowjob scene for the sequel, even though it'll never happen.

Preggo vids will make you a mint, if you know how to film with maternal sensibilities. Unfortunately, Elvira isn't packing any embryos.

Bird's-eye shot:

Ninio straightens his back, pushes his head up, and thrusts the rest of his meat into Elvira. One lurch is all it takes. The camera catches a touch of moongleam in his eye. He's there.

Extreme close-up:

Ninio pulls out and dismounts. Semen and paraurethral fluid gush out of Elvira's pussy, splattering the lens. It's all good in the new school of cinematography. Then she pisses a river, Ninio sucks a few litres into his trunk, and he sprinkles it over them both.

But it's not the fancy-footed grip work, or the incontinence, or the near-constant zoom-ins on Elvira's rawhide pubes that will make this film a bestseller. It's the last clip-art bubble:

"Gay icon? I don't think so."

We're looking at a street-corner smash, and maybe even a Zoomie nomination.

CAPTAIN JACK BONAVITA

To the Gentlemen of the Great West Life Insurance Company, Esteem'd Claims Officers:

It was, no doubt, with Consternation and Regret that you learned of the Fire at Dreamland Amusement Park, that besmirch'd Day of 27 May. 'Tis a Day, to be sure, that I should wish to wipe clean from my Mem'ry, were it not for certain pressing monetary Considerations that I must call to your Attention. Allow me, Men of Finance, to proceed with a brief retelling of His Almighty's inscrutable Whims on the Night previous to said Day.

In accordance with our Policy of mark'd continual Improvement, and to restore Coney Island to the Heights of Fantazy and Rantipole (a Challenge our honourable Competitors at Luna Park failed mizerably to achieve), the Directors of Dreamland assessed, in sage Turns, the Need for last-minute Renovations. These were carried out dutifully on the Night of 26 May. In great Anticipation of Opening Day the following Morning, Labourers set upon the Hell's Gate Concession to caulk it capably with Buckets of hot Pitch.

As you surely have heard from my Colleagues, between Sunfall and Sunrize, an Occurrence of unparalleled Misfortune happen'd. 'Twould appear as tho' the Lightbulbs began to pop in a pell-mell Fashion. The Building caught Fire instantly, and the Flames spread with Haste to nearby Constructions. Notwithstanding the 1,750 Tonnes of Asbestos and other fireproofing Materials, the Amusements burn'd for their frames of Plaster and Lath.

'Twas to fight the devilish Conflagration of the Dreamland Tower that Fire Companies from across the Borough arriv'd to join the Combatants already assembled, and all of Brooklyn turn'd up to watch from the Sidelines. In the Blink of an Eye, numerous Assets were consum'd, among them *Chilkoot Pass, Canals of Venice, Revels of Japan, Coasting through Switzerland, Destruction of Pompeii, Shoot-the-Chutes, Parisian Novelty,* and *Hiram Maxim's Airships.* A formidable Twist of Irony can be observed in that not even those in the Employ of the *Fighting the Flames* Concession were able to tame a single Lick of Flame with their Fire Hoses.

Compassionate Gentlemen, no Horror can compare to that experienced by the Beasts shelter'd in the Animal Arena. To circumvent the Rise of a general Panic among the Antelope, Lynx, Wolves, Bears, Lions, Zebras, and Baboons, I, in my Wisdom, freed them from their Cages and kept them trotting in the Roundabout with smart Cracks of the Whip. Only Little Hip, the darling Elephant whose Antics are regal'd as far away as Manhattan, refus'd to leave his Cage. I implore the Officers of the reputable Great West Life Insurance Company to note that I took all reasonable Actions to coax out this Prize of my Coterie, to no Avail.

Little Hip witnessed the Dreamland Tower fall upon the other Animals as in the frightful Reverie in the Book of Revelation, Chapter 16, Verse 8, which you well remember from your Catechisms: "And the fourth Angel poured out his Vial upon the Sun; and the power was granted unto him to scorch the Men with Fire." That day, the Wickedness of Mankind brought a Scourge likewise to innocent Beasts, and Sorrow into my Bosom, I assure you.

The Shetland Ponies and Victoria, the Pregnant Lion, managed to run to Safety. Disaster, however, showed its ghastly Face when the scarlet Fire envelop'd the hapless Zebras and Lions, who scattered with Manes aflame through the crisped Gates of Dreamland, sounding their Death-Screams askance into Brooklyn, seven of them in total.

We are here put in mind of Revelation, Chapter 17, Verse 3: "I saw a woman sitting on a scarlet-coloured beast full of names of blasphemy. It had seven heads and ten horns."

The Platypusses, sick Aberrations of Faunae that they are, were braised uniformly out of this World by the Grace of God. To prevent further Displays of this shocking Nature, I mercifully produc'd Lead Bullets from my Pistol into the Skulls of the Horses, Pumas, Hyenas, and, yes, the remaining Lions, bringing their Nightmare to a Close.

Only Little Hip, judicious Officers, would I not shoot. Surrounded by inescapable Heat, he trumpeted his last Breaths with great Noise before bravely succumbing to Hades. After a careful Examination of the Facts, you will no doubt ascertain that I employed all measures within my Power to preserve the Life of this expensive Attraction, as the Pachyderm is not obtained cheaply through any of the common Asian or African Routes.

Gentlemen of the Great West Life Insurance Company, it is with this Letter and the faithfully enclosed Receipt that I justify my Claim of $723.18 for said Elephant. Far be it from my Intentions to amend our Contract with a Coddleshell, but I have also attached Documents that demonstrate the current Tusk and Penis market Value, vis-à-vis a post-mortem Standpoint.

May Mankind never again witness such a Tragedy, we pray.

Only you have the Wherewithal to compensate for what the Lord has wrought on this wretched Creature.

Truthfully Yours,
Captain Jack Bonavita
Animal Trainer

TINNITUS

The bells had already started to ring.

I was in the back seat of a cab in Nowa Huta, headed to the Człowiek Obcy Gallery for the Great Fire of London when the radio announcer delivered the news in a broken voice.

Panie i Panowie, umarł Papież

The driver stopped the car in the middle of the street. It was night. The radio fought with the bells for our attention.

Panie i Panowie, umarł Papież

Panie i panowie, Papież nie Żyje

Maybe he knew his listeners needed to hear it from different grammatical angles for it to sink in. But we had all known this was coming. The commentator could've said it any way he liked, and it wouldn't have changed a thing.

A flash mob blocked the street, and the driver hit the brakes. It was easy to see the masses of people in the dark because they were phosphorescent. They moved as a single entity, slowly, protecting tiny fires and spreading them from hand to hand. They carried lit candles plucked from dinner tables and birthday cakes and emergency kits, and windproof candles in red plastic cups that they had no doubt hoarded for occasions like this. The driver backed up to the last intersection and rerouted the trip. I was going to be late for my show, not that it mattered.

The bells were gonging wildly, but there was no melody. The dissonance spread over the roofs, one church catching it from the other, until all Kraków was sonic chaos. People poured out of restaurants still chewing their last bites, and stumbled out of hair salons with lopsided bobs. Supermarket staff crawled into the store windows, tearing down advertisements and crying into the wadded up, high-gloss paper.

Kurva.

We came to another impasse, still stuck in Nowa Huta. A crowd gathered around Arka Pana—The Lord's Ark—the first church in our dear Soviet suburb. The driver could've jumped the parking lot median and slipped out the exit on the other side of the crush, but it was clear he wanted to watch for a few minutes.

Watch, I thought, but told him, "Go."

[It is midnight, 1960, in the City without God. Bishop Karol Wojtyła stands in a barren field, his arms stretched heavenward, giving a midnight Christmas mass to no one, speaking the liturgy in foggy puffs. Behind him, the residents of Nowa Huta are afraid and peer furtively from the windows of their apartment blocks. The bishop knows that the cold may paralyze his throat and that the police may ask him to leave. Still, he continues.]

Tinnitus is often described as a ringing in the ear corresponding to no external sound, but it can be much more. It can be the slooshing of the ocean or an insistent breeze, the chirping of a grasshopper you can't seem to kill. It can also be much less: an occasional click. Church bells can touch off a variety of sounds, long after they quit swinging.

But the bells were still raising thunder, and we darted down a side street to look for another way downtown. People were now draping their windowsills with yellow and white Vatican flags garnished with a single black ribbon to signify mourning. Behind the flags, pictures of Karol Wojtyła ripped from photo albums and picture frames and *magazyny*, printed dot matrix from the Internet, and painted lovingly in oils. Few pictures showed him wearing vestments; now that he was dead, he was allowed to be human again. People were allowed to scream and tear the hair off their arms and beat recycling boxes with trash cans.

You could tell that they had been craving this national communion for decades.

The Polish word *osoby* has a much different feeling than its English equivalent, "people." It's more of a collective than a collection. So tough to explain.

[Midnight Mass, 1966. Still outside in the field, but somewhat formalized with a portable podium and altar, and a microphone and speakers hooked up to a diesel generator. Archbishop Wojtyła no longer addresses only God, speaking instead to the thousands assembled before him. "*Nie bój się. Nie lękajcie się!*" But Nowa Huta is long past the point of fear, now that the community has hired a professional architect to draft blueprints for an illegal church. "It is real now that it is on paper," says a man in the crowd.

"No," the Archbishop counters, "it is real when you gather out here in the cold. You are the rock on which Peter built his church."

"Peter's rock is a political machine, and it is going to crush their skulls," the man says, blowing cigarette smoke into the sky. This mass is being hijacked by people who would later become members of the *Solidarność* movement. They were hoping to give each other the best Christmas present ever—a revolution.

Now we were parked in the middle of Tyniecka Street, surrounded by *osoby* gathered to see the house where Karol once hid from the Nazis.

Witaj Królowo nieba i Matko litości

Witaj nadziejo nasza, w smutku i żałości

You typically heard this chant when your *babcia* died. Your family would go hoarse repeating it, to keep the sobs at bay. Swallow. You heard this when sadness and emphysema took your *dziadek*, when they told you, in every possible grammatical way, so there would be no confusion. Exhale.

But I never heard this hymn when my mother died. As a matter of fact, I didn't hear a fucking thing in the days and weeks and years that followed.

It sounded as if Radio Maryja had turned its mics to the window to broadcast the sound of mourners spilling into the streets in greater numbers, shuffling, roaming aimlessly. Refrains dropped off and resumed again out of nowhere. The sound of thirty-eight million people destined to get lost in each other's grief.

The announcer didn't dare play any recorded music. Who could presume to choose the right soundtrack for a night like this?

"Turn here," I told the driver. We were in Kraków, but still nowhere near the gallery. The meter was running up a fortune, and with this one deft move, I knew we could bypass St Stanislaus, St Michael, St Florian, St Francis of Assisi, the Papal Stone of the Blonia Commons, and anywhere else troublemakers were likely to gather that night.

"That will be worse," he said, glancing at me in a rearview mirror choked with plastic rosaries. "You're telling me we'll be able to get within a kilometre of St Mary's Basilica?"

He had a point. It's national lore that when young Karol finished a work day at the quarry mines, he would stop by St Mary's to soak up the stained glass. It's no secret he was a Queen of Poland junkie.

"Just do something," I said. "We can't go straight."

"Why not, Mr GPS?" The driver was miffed, and popped the clutch on purpose, jerking us both forward.

"Because that's where the Solvay chemical factory was," I said. Where Karol had bottled poison as a young man. Kraków is crows, but it's also nostalgia. We were navigating through a landmine of sacred sites.

"Give me a better reason."

"Because you're not getting a fucking *grosz* from me if you go straight."

"Then I'll take you right to the police station."

It was 8:45. If my gallery audience hadn't dispersed into the slipstream of mourners, they would still be waiting for me to set London ablaze. Frustration was making me peel my lips with my teeth.

It wasn't the taxi driver that was getting to me. It was the noise. You could hear that this death was going to change things permanently.

Medically speaking, subjective tinnitus makes no sense.

Researchers give these sufferers of phantom crickets and whistles a sample sound to listen to, a gauge to measure the buzz that's slowly driving them *zwariowane*. Here lies the contradiction: patients focusing on the sample can often hear it below five decibels, rendering their internal hummingbirds and cicadas undetectable, but when focussing on the tinnitus and ignoring the sample, the same *osoby* claim insect symphonies of seventy decibels—as loud as a vacuum cleaner.

Do you see what I mean? Tinnitus is impossible to measure.

It may sound strange, but even with this din, there was still too much silence in my life. Missing speech. To this day, it kills me not to know all that my mother screamed from the fire. "Tell him." Maybe she's behind every inferno I plan, a wraith wrapped in a bed sheet, a spook in a shawl of embers. Invisible and mute, with a swatch of duct tape over her mouth. It's almost as if I'm waiting for her to make an appearance and to shout a little louder this time. What did she want to tell me? I'm a child in Lourdes, with my sister, waiting for Mother Mary to materialize in a rainbow blur and take us by surprise. But most of all, I need to know if we're alone in this world. I need to know if the apparition can ever happen or if it's just a stupid dream.

And I need to know if the sister—Dorota, I mean—is for real.

Do we really need relationships if they end up causing us agony? It wouldn't surprise me to learn that they're merely conversations with fellow travellers carried on for far too long.

[Nowa Huta, 1983. Karol Wojtyła is speaking in the middle of a field, where he did so for over a decade. But the middle of the field is now Kościół Arka Pana, a big ship of a church with a cross for a mast, built exactly according to blueprint. The Lord's Ark, like the Elephant House, is shaped like a flying saucer but is an ocean-going vessel, with a four-metre metal Jesus figurehead arching his giant chest forward into the waves. The church is packed, and 250,000 more believers wait outside for a glimpse of Karol. Little has changed, except that he's now Pope and has just unknowingly kissed a man dying of AIDS, giving him a personal sacrament. HIV now courses through Poland, but the general public won't know this for years. And even when they find out, nobody will get tested or administer the tests. Nobody sees the pinpricks that old shopkeepers poke into condoms to give sperm a chance in a cruel world out to get them. The cameras, however, catch the Pope's every hand gesture as he consecrates the first church in the City without God. Peter is pulverizing the Communists, one construction site at a time. Karol is definitely more useful to the Solidarity movement as Pope than as Karol.]

It was 9:15, and I was furious that London—that heathen, roiling, plague-filled heap of lumber—was spared the dignities of fire. One of the greatest in history, according to the effusive museum paintings usually done in flourishes of yellow, crimson, and hell.

The driver, I realized, had no intention of getting me to the gallery. He had been making a sacred-site pilgrimage this entire time, praying for gridlock and bilking me through the nose.

I paid the ridiculous fare, got out of the cab, and froze in the glow of the intersection. The traffic was wedged in the vertices of a cross made of thousands of candles stretching from sidewalk to sidewalk ... to sidewalk to sidewalk. I knew it was only one of hundreds that were guttering throughout Kraków at that precise moment, drawing devotees of the Virgin Mary closer, like flies.

Everybody wants to see a vision of their Mother.

It was too much.

Tinnitus, it turns out, isn't always imaginary. Pulsatile tinnitus occurs when increased blood flow to the ear causes audible—and verifiable—spasms and clicks.

Sometimes we just want to hear these sounds, whether they're real or not.

Clang, clang.

YOUTUBE

The Amphitheatre of Pompeii, 1971.

Slow zoom in from the highest rung of stone seating to the centre of the circular arena. From far away, we see four figures hunched in front of giant speakers. Dust hangs in the blinding sunlight, cutting a mid-air shade unevenly. As the camera gets closer, we see that the four figures are playing to technicians tweaking knobs on a network of soundboards.

A horizontal tracking shot across equipment cases:

PINK FLOYD, LONDON

Pan to a sleepy Mount Vesuvius in the background. Pink Floyd has travelled to the oldest surviving Roman amphitheatre to perform for an audience of their own roadies.

In the name of art? Hardly.

"Chapter 24," from their album *The Piper at the Gates of Dawn*, is the first song on the set list, although it never made it onto the officially released film. Don't ask me how I found it.

The narrator chatters: "On August 24, in the year 79 CE, Vesuvius spewed pumice and ash for a solid day, burying the city under a twenty-metre blanket. This was the day after Vulcanalia, festival for the Roman god of fire."

Roger Waters chugs through bass notes that echo on the slate slabs of the amphitheatre. Close-up stock footage of lava bubbling and boiling, while Nick Mason hits the cymbals, synching up to the imagery far too precisely. The microphone catches wind and adds a new layer of fuzz to the distortion.

The lyrics echo the words of the I Ching, the Chinese Book of Changes, supposedly describing the steps involved in performing a divination:

> Six in the third place means
> The image of the Turning Point
> Six at the top means
> Misfortune from within and without.

At Pompeii, however, on instruments that shatter in sunbursts of every colour, we see a different interpretation. It's obvious that the Floyd are singing about the stages of a developing flame. The band hasn't even played the first bridge of the song yet, and we see pangs of the first three: red becoming visible (525°C), cherry dull (800°C), and cherry clear (1,000°C).

Rick Wright is fucking the Farfisa organ, and we can tell by the kryptic look on his face that he's leaning into chords entirely new to him. Professional recording is the best time to improvise, because you can always rewind the tape if you forget the finger steps.

Cross-fade to footage of stone gargoyles found at the Pompeii ruins. The facial grimaces are perfectly preserved. Whose faces?

Orange deep (1,100°C) and orange clear (1,200°C), the fourth and fifth stages. A cloud passes, and the drum kit shines. The hotter it gets, the shorter the Celsius increments.

The city was uncovered nearly 1,700 years after the eruption, when archaeologists found curious pockets in the solidified ash. They twigged on the human shapes of these holes, injected them with plaster, and made casts of Pompeiani frozen in their last moments of life.

Coiled bodies in situ, fear etched into furrowed foreheads.

Nick Mason breaks a drumstick and expertly replaces it before the next cymbal crash.

At five kilometres away from the volcano, magma didn't get the Pompeiians and neither did fire. Wisps of pyroclast are harmless, but when they snowball into an avalanche, there's nowhere to run. Ash is a nightmare.

> Six in the third place means
> The image of the Turning Point
> Six at the top means
> Misfortune from within and without

Bright white (1,400°C) is the sixth stage.

Dolly shot of the camera circling the band. They seem to be getting tired in the heat, maybe sick of playing to a phantom crowd. They slog on with the song, but now it looks automatic. Roger Waters' face is an oily pizza. Any bursts of energy are probably just retakes carefully spliced together. Two guys, probably bored sound engineers, sit together under an umbrella drinking cans of San Pellegrino soda.

Archaeologists were surprised to unearth erotic frescoes at Pompeii. The video clips are littered with black censor bars, but they outline must-see body parts rather exquisitely:

> A woman sprawled on a pile of crêpe fabric, with a centurion diligently eating out her cunt.

> A bearded man with wolverine legs fucking a goat. The animal is in full revolt.

A woman doing the "reverse cowgirl" over another woman's hand. There's a Mona Lisa thing going on, because we can see traces of her face, beneath the fresco, where she was once facing her fisting partner.

A mural of Priapus and his giant cock were not found until 1998, after a heavy rainfall washed away the mud that was covering it.

The sun wanes, and "Chapter 24" is nearing its finish, but this raging 1,400°C is by no means the end. A technician turns on a light rig and floods the band with 1,500°C dazzling white: the seventh stage of fire. Pink Floyd have had a good week. The *Book of Changes* agrees:

> On the seventh day comes return
> It furthers one to have somewhere to go.

David Gilmour plays a plangent guitar note and hits the whammy bar to make it cry. Why does he have to ruin everything? He doesn't even belong in this song.

Nobody ever mentions Herculaneum, the narrator complains, the other city that Vesuvius destroyed.

Zoom in on a piece of tourist graffiti:

SODOM AND GOMORRAH, YOU HAD IT COMING

Cut to the opening bars of "Set the Controls for the Heart of the Sun."

FOOTBALL

After the closing night of my London show at Człowiek Obcy (we rescheduled the vernissage fire), I came home on the *tramwaj* and looked forward to a relaxing night of vegging. Is that the expression? "Vegging"? I've always wondered what you thought of my English.

My rest was postponed, however, when I got distracted by a pile of junk in front of my building. Garbage piles never last long in Nowa Huta.

There's a belief that runs through the neighbourhood, learned under Communism, that everything can be salvaged. To the seasoned scavenger, a busted baby carriage isn't trash. It's a set of wheels that can be refitted on a shopping buggy, a mash of metal to turn into curtain rods along with fabric to hang on them. It's a display case of merchandise with a sign that says, "Steal me."

I saw too much good stuff to pass up: T-shirts that were mouldy but in fun styles, a beheaded oscillating fan that looked a lot like mine, and a television tube, intact but separated from its smashed casing. I was visualizing how I could paint the tube orange and use it in my next maquette to give San Francisco a ghoulish glow from a hole cut in the Mission District. But I lost that train of thought completely when I saw *The Final Cut*.

This Pink Floyd album was arguably a Roger Waters solo project with the odd contribution by other band members. How could it not be their greatest album?

Then a few of my books hit the pile.

I looked up to see Pan Laskiewicz, that twitchy mongrel, chucking my shit over the balcony. I raced into the building, taking the stairs two at a time, and trying desperately to remember what I knew about criminal law and bodily assault.

When I reached my apartment, a set of keys were in the lock, and the door was open.

I saw his back first, and got a tiger-like instinct to jump him from behind and core his brain like an apple. In his hand, I saw a white-rimmed black triangle that refracted into the colour spectrum: my mint LP copy of *Dark Side of the Moon*. But I was crunching loudly toward him over my ransacked stuff, and he heard me, ruining my surprise attack.

"Aha!" he said, his face alive with glee. "You have come a little too late to assist with your own eviction. I have been given this most wonderful task."

Pan Laskiewicz showed me the official *eksmisji prawna*, apparently signed by my enemy, the *urzędnik*. It had to be a forgery; in Nowa Huta, bureaucracy was as slow as *melasa*.

"Get the fuck out of my house," I told him, "before I throw you over the railing."

"Oh, the homosexual is getting angry! I considered taking the stairs to move your stuff out, but this is much more fun. No nail polish today, my *pedał*?"

With that, he dropped the album over the balcony and sealed the deal.

Nobody messes with my Dutch pressings.

I dragged him back into the apartment by his arm hair and kneed him in the chest. He was winded for a few seconds, but sprang right back. He was pretty ripped for a guy in his fifties and tried to choke. Me. Against. The. Ironing. Board. Built. Into. The. Wall. Until I broke free and successfully jammed one of his fingers into the mechanism, then closed the ironing board.

A clean slice, and he lost it. Not the finger, but almost.

His index finger ripening blue and nasty, Pan Laskiewicz opened his maw and sank his yellowed tusks into my face, snorting through his whiskers. A wild djik—I had always known his true identity.

The apartment was coffee breath and pain for a spell. I lost a few seconds to dimness, almost blacking out. Then I staggered over to the mirror so I could see my wound, but there was no mirror, just a nail in the wall.

"You're going down, piece of shit," I told him.

"Is this making you excited? Do you want to suck my cock?" He mimed unzipping his pants and stroking himself.

Then I kicked his nose.

Heard the bone snap, the crunch of cartilage.

"No," he said.

He dropped to the ground to cradle the new sinkhole in his face. I crouched beside him. Half of his nose, it seemed, had disappeared into him. He fondled bits of broken bone like a rosary, rocking back and forth. It was too much for me to take, especially with a bite gash in my face. I could hardly breathe.

"Pan Laskiewicz, I'm so sorry."

"All I wanted," he cried and blew bubbles in blood, "was to see you fuck my wife." He looked up at me pleadingly with eyes quickly swelling black. "Was that such a ridiculous [he had a hard time saying it] demand?"

My last experience in that apartment—and in sweet, miserable Nowa Huta—was tousling his black locks of hair. I noticed streaks of grey for the first time, and how his hair smelled of vanilla and nutmeg. I vowed never to forget the soft side of this man, or of any enemy, for that matter.

Then I grabbed a few empty laundry bags and packed what I thought was important from the apartment and from the heap near the street. It was surprisingly easy to figure out; books were the only things I wanted, and I packed more than I could comfortably carry.

I left my records behind because I was done with music for awhile. I know—it's hard to believe. But something had changed in me, I could tell, the instant I broke Pan Laskiewicz's nose. Something let go. My choice in psychedelic rock bands simply didn't articulate my rage anymore, and they became quite useless to me.

Sheer fucking heresy. That's what this country will do to you.

I headed down Solidarności Boulevard hunting for a cab to Dorota's house but couldn't find one, so I walked the few kilometres there. The city was still under a funereal lock-down. Candles in colourful plastic shells lit my way. Shades were drawn in nearly every window, children cycled by me wearing commemorative black armbands, and stop signs were plastered with photos of the pontiff. Trams weren't running. The billboard at the Rondo Mogilskie, the one that had been advertising tampons for months, had been scraped clean. I guess feminine hygiene was deemed too vile a subject to acknowledge at such a "holy" time.

Maybe the eviction notice *wasn't* a forgery. Maybe the Pope's death, only a few days prior, had sped up the eviction process, especially where a fag like me was concerned.

SAN FRANCISCO

Dorota has generously given me the living room in her apartment.
There's more floor space than furniture, so I can build San Francisco
without having to stand in Buena Vista Park. The wall-to-wall books
are inspiring. She has such fine taste.

Focussing on a disaster like San Francisco helps me forget my own
piles of rubble.

Fresh *koperek*. Dill, to you. Dorota has been cooking all day, filling
the house with the fragrance of one comforting hint after another.
She bangs her wooden spoon hard on the side of a pot. We've developed many wordless forms of communication like this, because
Kraków has become too drowned in words, endless spoken noise
about the Pope's funeral, the pilgrimages to St Peter's Basilica to see
his remains lying in state, who will replace him, the white smoke, the
black smoke, the cardinals are in disarray, his life was a model for all,
Santo Subito, there's another memorial at the Franciscan Church, *Santo
Subito*, the children loved him, *Santo Subito*, he cannot be replaced, *Santo
Subito*, make him a saint right now.

We couldn't hear each other.

The clang from the kitchen means the *żurek* is simmering according
to plan. She's rolling cabbage heads across the counter and causing
a ruckus: *bigos* is definitely on the way. I can't wait. I might have to

remove my facial bandage to get my chops wet.

The San Francisco "Fire" of 1906 wasn't a fire, according to the history books, it was an earthquake. The San Andreas Fault maintains a cultural dictatorship over all kinds of writing, I'm told.

I'm using styrofoam to get the hills just right. I can see how buildings had a hard time standing on this roller-coaster terrain, and probably still do.

San Francisco will be destroyed so thoroughly that it doesn't matter what I build. The quake will level most of the city, then thirty natural gas fires will start and eventually merge into one. Firefighters will dynamite untouched buildings to create a firebreak, causing fifty percent more damage than the fire alone would have caused.

Still haven't found a popsicle-brick façade suited to this cautionary note:

DON'T FALL IN LOVE WITH BUILDINGS. THEY'LL
ONLY BREAK YOUR HEART

I'm hungry and having difficulty concentrating. Food has always relaxed me. Dorota senses my condition and brings me a snack of open-faced, cheese-spread sandwiches sprinkled with green onion and a side of cubed rzodkiewki. I mean radishes. I'm sick of translating for you, so I probably won't do it anymore. Anyway, if you can't handle Polish food in its native tongue, then you're certainly not ready to try naleśniki jagodowe, mielony ziemniakami, pierogi z kapusta i grzybami, barszcz czerwony, pstrąg, galaretka owocowa, or zupa rybna. You might never be ready for a hunk of golonka, or to adopt the habit of having dessert before dinner.

My heart isn't in this project, because it's such a fake. Most San Francisco insurance companies refused to cover earthquake damage, so people torched their houses on purpose to get the money. The army had orders to shoot looters, and soldiers gunned down 500 people. The thing is, most of them were try to salvage stuff from their own homes. This "Great Fire," unlike all others, pisses me off.

Will gallery attendees notice if I leave Buena Vista Park flat, without a hill?

Barely audible, but she was grinding pepper.

It gets worse. Days after the fire was out, idiots across the city opened their combination safes—still warm to the touch—to see if their valuables were intact. The fire tetrahedron got its oxygen fix when air rushed into the fireproof chambers and incinerated their documents. A phenomenon known as backdraft.

Good for them.

I need to take a chill tablet.

I've assembled a row of Pacific Heights brownstones but plopped them down in the wrong end of town, in a puddle of glue I don't see the point in displacing. Wonderful. I have no idea what I'm do-ing. What was I hoping to accomplish with these maquettes, these juvenile pieces of junk? They don't cause enough trouble to be mean-ingful. Either I upgrade to real arson or quit fire altogether, because I haven't done a single thing to change life for queers in Poland.

Remember what I said about Christo and Jeanne-Claude? Maybe I'm looking for change in the wrong places. Maybe I'm thinking too small.

Dorota sets the table, arranging plates of chleb, masło, and porzeczki jam just so. But I'm losing my appetite.

You have to know about the vile mythology coming out of San Francisco. There's a fire hydrant on the corner of 20th and Church Streets that was allegedly the only one still functioning after the water mains had broken. It saved half the city, and now residents gather every year to paint it gold.

Spare us the story, please. That hydrant, if it isn't a fraud installed after the fact, saved the Mission Dolores—a church. *That's all*. Fire creates too many legends we can't back up, and then the legends breed in church basements where we can't stamp them out.

For spite, I've left the Golden Hydrant off the grid. I'm acting unprofessional, and I don't give a shit.

Armed with a can of Krylon gold, I spray a warning across the entire city, like poison gas:

DON'T FALL IN LOVE WITH FIRES, START THEM

The warning is for me.

"It's ready," Dorota says. She has spoken too much. I'm still angry. We eat in silence.

DEAR BOYFRIEND

Lovely Radeki,

It is so special to have you in my house, though I regret not being able to give you better accommodations. Anyhow, I hope you are comfortable. There are clean towels in the linen closet.

Do you know how much my life has changed since you came into it? Of course you don't, because I have never told you. Radek: you have unravelled me. Sometimes I just sit here and cry, thinking about the Poland you envision. Will we ever get it? It doesn't show (because I don't let it), but I have a mini-breakdown on every one of our adventures. For an instant, I fall into a gloom that makes me cold all over. Then something you say revives me, and I want to cry with happiness. You bring my emotions full circle.

I try not to expose you to this because I don't want to distract you from your work. But now you know.

Thank you for your letters.

They released a lot of blocked tears and have given me insight into the man you are today: kind, gentle, searching. It's so tempting for a girl like me who grew up in the university (my parents are both professors) to assume I know what you need. To slot you into an archetype and say, "This will be your downfall." But if I believe all that schooling, dear boyfriend, I will lose hope, and I can't do that. Please understand that I have never played anthropologist with you. You have made me queer by teaching me that there are alternative options—for straight girls, too. Jagielloński will never give me that. (Don't worry—if I drop out, I'll make sure not to lose any credits.)

I keep thinking about the flashlight and the book. Your fire. I wish I had been there to hold your hand in the street. I cannot imagine the pain you have been holding inside all these years. Some days, I can almost see the hole in your chest, but I blind myself to it. I refuse to see you as a broken person.

Your last letter really shocked me, because it doesn't sound like you. I must say that I find your idea of striking St Mary's Basilica incredibly foolish.

Yes, a fire there would "carve the liver right out of the country," as you wrote in the letter. My mind wanders to what you see: flames lighting up the blue panes of stained glass and the giant gold altarpiece. "A Gothic treat in a single swallow." What you meant is an instant equalizer. You're such an artist, I swear, and that's why you never say what you mean.

In theory, I understand why this target makes sense to you. The church fought viciously for freedom from the Communists, but now refuses to grant gays and queers the simplest of freedoms. I hate the church as much as you do, but that's the problem I see with this plan.

(I'm sorry I over-salted your *kotlet mielony* yesterday. It won't happen again.)

An act of hatred, Radeki, will only draw more hatred toward us. Also, isn't it pointless to burn down symbols so tied to the country's history of rebellion—as an *act of rebellion*? Solidarity was born in the shipyards but grew up in the pews. A church fire would send such a mixed message. And please think of the physical danger: would you be able to escape in time? In the Middle Ages, a bugler would stand on the roof of St Mary's and blow his horn to warn of fire and attacks. Would he have thought about looking for smoke below him? Would any of us?

Besides, it's such a beautiful building. There are uglier churches in the city, you know. And I'm starting to wonder if fire is only regenerative and useful when it happens spontaneously.

My sweet one, I understand your need to gain closure regarding your mother, but I suspect you're hoping to actually see her in the flames. Is that true? Radeki, people spend decades saying their Hail Marys, and they still never see the Virgin Mother. What makes you think you'll see yours? I'm not trying to be mean. We can talk more about this in person.

Surprise time: I have purchased a copy of *The Legend of the Smok Wawelski*. Yes, the rare, Russian-issue first edition! It's not easy to find Soviet memorabilia on eBay, but I managed. The spelling mistakes have made this book quite expensive, but it's so worth it. I have placed it under the pillow in your sleeping bag because the book is rich in dreams, and you need to stay close to your subconscious these days. It might help you.

I would love to heal you with my own poetry one day, but I truly wonder if I'll ever write anything worthwhile. I appear to be made of school, not neologisms.

Here's a clipping you might like:

"Speaking with European Union officials in Brussels, Jarosław Kaczyński said: 'I ask you not to believe in the myth of Poland as a homophobic and xenophobic country ... People with such [homosexual] preferences have full rights in Poland; there is no tradition of persecuting such people.'"

Well. Jarek had *better* hope that gays have full rights in Poland, especially now that he's been outed on the radio :)

What's with those Kaczyński brothers?

Dear boyfriend, we may not have much time before the government, with the help of the church, crushes us completely. But we will have to use something stronger than fire. We will use the Internet.

I'll tell you more about it on the train tomorrow.

Now, let me ask you a few questions about the Smok Wawelski: why would the dragon prefer virgins? It baffles me. Wouldn't a girl be more succulent with the additional vaginal mucus that comes with sex? And where would a ten-year-old boy get a calling card before the printing press was invented? Very funny. I've read the original version of *The Legend*, and I can see that you've re-imagined it much differently. Your version is *ekstra*.

I've taken the liberty of rewriting the ending. No offence. And I added a bit more dialogue because I was struck by *inspiracja*. (I agree that some things sound stupid in English.)

Chapter 3

The King realized that knights, princes, and other wastrels were impotent against the dragon. He was on the verge of giving up when a most powerful weapon skipped into his quarters: fifteen-year-old Stefcia, a nymphet in full bloom. She promised the King that she would be able to kill the dragon, "no problemo."

"I don't believe you," the King said.

"Piece of *ciastko*. I'll need thirty days alone with him, and someone to bring me books and meals and fresh clothes."

"Foolish chickadee. He'll munch you in a second!"

"Not with this," Stefcia said, pulling a square of fibrous, handmade paper out of her dress, flicking nipples already swollen with excitement. Dragon-hunting, it would appear, was her thing.

"Paper," his Majesty croaked. "You're an idiot."

"Are you really a king?" Stefcia asked, narrowing her eyes. "Where's your crown?"

"Never mind that. How will paper save my kingdom?"

"First of all," Stefcia said, "I'm foremost saving my ass, and then your stupid kingdom. Secondly, written on this paper is a secret that will change the way business is done, not only in caves but in castles as well."

"What's the secret?"

"It's for dragons only."

"Okay. Go ahead and try, but mark my words: there shall be no funeral for you."

So brave Stefcia marched straight to the Smocza Jama and knocked on the cave wall with a discarded femur. "Hello?" The startled dragon ran to the mouth of the cave and opened his cage-like jaw over her head. "Uh, you don't want to do that," she said, and waved her piece of paper. The dragon ignored her and wrapped his pulpy lips around her ears.

"LISTEN!" she screamed.

The dragon stepped back and obeyed.

"On this paper I have the secret to how dragons can live forever. But you cannot kill me until I read it to you, and you cannot leave the cave to eat or drink, in case I read it while you're gone." Stefcia fixed his gaze with her own. "I will read the secret only once."

So, the dragon camped in front of Stefcia while she read her books. He waited patiently, scrutinizing every movement of her delicious mouth for the moment when she would reveal the key to his immortality. Days passed, and she remained silent, taking her meals, bathing in the Wisła River, weaving daisy chains, and finger-painting on her naked body with pollen. The dragon studied her curves and clefts, salivating, imagining the hiding places where she kept the paper tucked away. But he kept his hunger in check, determined to hear the secret.

Ten days passed.

Twenty days passed.

Between chapters, Stefcia brewed tea with fresh chrysan-

themums, dipped her toes in the river, and looked for
words spelled out in the nighttime stars.

Thirty days passed. Still no secret.

[Watercolour illustration of the Smok Wawelski, dead
at Stefcia's feet. The corpse is shaded impeccably: scales
pulled taut over his hollowed-out face, his parched, leath-
ery tongue spread across her toes like a piece of roadkill.
Green evaporated into halos of carbonic black. Stefcia, it
appears, is still reading.]

CONCH

I just figured out how Radek rides PKP express trains for half-price: He buys a local fare (for much cheaper) and when he hands his ticket to the ticket-taker, he presses a nail-polished thumb over the incriminating section. Of course, they never ask him to move it.

No other thumb would work, not even mine. It's homosexual genius at its best.

Radek is so handsome. I'm not sure you care, but he has puppy-dog eyes like Elvis, and shaves twice a day to keep his face smooth. He has one dimple, a swirl of *koperek* I've wanted to lick for some time, and a permanent case of bed-head that makes me think about ... his bed.

We were headed to the Baltic Sea again, passing one dreary town after another, and antique tractors and homemade pigeon coops and seas of radishes and potatoes. Radek was fascinated and stared out the window, his chin lit by sunlight. We passed all his favourite animals: pigs were snuffling truffles out of the muddy soil, dogs were chasing foxes, and the sheep were doing nothing.

I unwrapped our lunch of hard-boiled eggs and a salad of peas and carrots, and I salted everything appropriately.

"Tell me about the Internet," Radek said.

"It's mostly online and written in code," I answered.

"I mean your plan, silly ... what's all this about?"

"This?"

"We're not going on an adventure, because we've been to Gdańsk before. Withholding information is a very Communist thing to do, you know."

"So people should constantly be spitting out their thoughts?" I said, suddenly not finding him very attractive. "They should speak without timing?"

"Of course not. But I'm ready to know."

I showed him my brand-new video camera.

"We're making a YouTube piece," I said.

"Actors?"

"You."

"Just me?"

"No, but you're the star."

"Pay?" He double salted his egg.

"Fame. I hope there are no zits on your ass cheeks."

"You can just pop them," he said. "You're pretty good at getting under the skin. Should I have brought condoms?"

"No."

We watched the countryside roll by.

"Thanks for the book," he said.

We got off in Gdańsk and had a cup of *herbatka* at the station restaurant. Then we pushed through the usual crowd of hooligans that clogged public places when school was out for the day, past juvenile comments about the size of my breasts and about Radek's nail polish. You know, "Who's the wife?" and other such childish remarks. Of course, I was the one who answered back, "Go fuck a pencil sharpener," because if Radek had said it, they would've beaten him up on the spot. You can't outrun a pack of kids on a 4 pm sugar high.

We caught our tramwaj to the beach. The weather was gorgeous. On our way to the bluffs, we passed a cluster of people setting up their picnic and arguing about the best way to get sand out of a cell phone. After we cleared them, Radek got naked immediately—even before I did—and I took it as a sign that the shoot would go well.

While we were walking through the bluffs to find a cozy spot, we came across patches of blood in the sand. People apparently had violent sex out here to a soundtrack of the sea ... I guess the water brings out something different in everyone.

We continued a little further and eventually settled on a bank of white sand flanked by reeds on three sides. We sat facing the beautiful, blue Baltic, at peace despite the broken shells and dead hermit crabs that poked through our towels and into our skin.

I leaned over to Radek, kissed him on his cherry lips, and then fell into his naked, cross-legged lap. He hovered over my face for a few seconds, inhaling my hair, and then he buried his tongue down my throat. Searching. He was always looking for something, this boy. We made out for a few minutes, then picked sand out of our mouths.

"Wow," he said. "Your molars taste metallic."

"That's because I have fillings. You're not supposed to notice."

That did it. My pussy was wet. Please understand, dear reader, if I need to use Radek's vulgar, Americanized English to explain what happened next.

He sniffed a noose around my neck and then turned idiot. He turned theoretical.

"Poland may learn to accept gays and lesbians in the coming decades, but it will take centuries for it to accept—"

"Be quiet," I interrupted. "I need your face near my pussy."

Radek obeyed. He lay on the sand in front of me, planted his face in my pubes, and took a deep whiff. His nostrils flared. This was about the body—our bodies—and not about "us," so I wasn't upset that he avoided eye contact with me. I preferred that sentimentality didn't ruin our session.

You see, Radek thinks I'm a nice girl, but I'm really an animal.

Who whitewashes a city of all tampon advertising for some guy's funeral? My vagina wasn't going to stand for invisibility. I lurched forward and fucked Radek's nose, smothering him with my labia. *Ekstra*, I thought. *His tongue knows what to look for and doesn't take long to find it.*

His tongue, in fact, was radically fudging up the gay community's spit-shined image of boy-on-boy, girl-on-girl. Bisexual stigma, lost right up my cunt.

I should've been enjoying these precious moments with Radek— the wind in his hair, the sun bronzing his pale ass, his tongue unleashing months of pent-up energy in me. Instead, I was thinking them to death.

"I almost forgot," I said, setting up the camera on a book beside us. "Let me just turn this on."

I rolled him over on his back and tried to quickly brush the sand off his cock, but it clung stubbornly to his moist foreskin. So I picked and picked. Then, when I thought it was clean, I pulled the skin back and found even more. The pee-hole is so interesting.

His erection grew in my hand, long and thick. Forcing my fingers apart. This was what I had been waiting for. Can a virgin be queer? Can a virgin be anything? I decided not to tell him this was my first time, in case it would spook the roughness out of him.

I straddled Radek's body, lifted up his heavy dick, and slowly impaled myself on it. This girl's tummy got very full, very fast. Anatomy doesn't make any sense when it's being turned inside out. Radek's face became a pool of pleasure, and then he throbbed, pulsing into me. I daydreamed his cockhead would erupt on his strongest throb, pushing blood into my deepest recesses.

I was silly with lust. Since when do I drool?

Then he flipped me on my back and pumped my pussy raw. Bits of shell were digging into me, but I didn't care.

Radek thought that nothing had changed, but that's not true. We had changed, and our bodies told us so.

"Fuck," I said. "You feel that?"

"Yeah, I'm in your fornix."

And with those words, I came and came and came, and squeezed the cum out of sweet Radeki, as orgasm deformed his face against a sky of squawking seagulls.

He collapsed beside me, then after a few minutes of rest, threw my ankles over my head and ate my ass out like a fucking pig. My anus was Queen of Poland for five minutes, and I came again.

Sigh.

Radek laid his head on my stomach and faced the water.

"You know what's hotter than a gay guy who knows where the fornix is?" I asked, the last full sentence I spoke to him that day. "A gay guy who can reach it."

He looked happy. I wanted so badly to go clean up in the sea with him, and then swim and play all day, but I was too tired to move.

"What does this have to do with the Internet?" Radek said.

I had forgotten all about the video camera. It was still recording.

"I'm going to post this online, with the caption 'If he's not afraid of pussy—'"

And that's when we saw the skinheads kicking their way through the bluffs, threshing the reeds with iron chains and laughing. It could only be one thing, the worst thing: They were on a faggot hunt.

I can still hear the swish of their track suits. It was the most terrifying sound ever.

But Radek was with me—a naked woman who smelled of sex—so I was sure he was safe.

The skinheads saw us, and the short, wiry one threw down his beer can. A stream of gold spilled into the sand and meandered toward us.

"What's up, bitch?"

"I'm with my boyfriend."

"This pedal?" he said, holding up Radek's hand. "Only women and perverts wear nail polish."

Radek froze, like a sculpture. I was expecting a little more fight in him, but he was naked and vulnerable. I forgive him.

"We just had sex," I said, and showed him Radek's cum leaking out of me.

"Who cares. He'll always be a faggot." He twisted Radek's wrist backwards for a few seconds and then threw his hand down. Not a yelp from my baby.

In any other situation, I would've agreed with the skinhead, because he was right. Radek was a free spirit who could identify however he wanted, and one fuck wasn't going to change that. But Radek's life, I realized, was now in my care.

"Why don't you leave him alone, and just fuck me."

"Does it look like we want AIDS?" the other thug said, fitting himself with a set of brass knuckles.

"If he's not afraid of pussy, then he's not afraid of you," I said desperately.

That was supposed to be the video caption.

And then Radek took off, dashing naked down the beach with

these two monsters running after him.

I forgive him.

It was going to be like old times, I thought, starting with a *franchissement*, then a *passe muraille*, followed by an acrobatic *roulade* into the water. I was certain Radek would kick gravity in the nuts, and transform into the superhero he was always meant to be.

But that's not how it went. He got a few hundred yards, then tripped in the sand and fell. The skinheads caught up with him. One of them held Radek down by pressing a boot on his neck, while the other fetched a nearby conch shell. Together, they pried opened his mouth, and gently placed the spire in the back of his throat.

I wish I had never seen that shell.

Parkour only works when there are obstacles to overcome. The beach is a horribly barren place.

I forgive him.

That's where the video ends, because I turned off the "record" function. This was only supposed to be a porn shoot, a picnic, a bonding experience. Unfortunately, it turned into so much more, especially after the short skinhead, the one with the venom in his leg, gave the first banana kick.

There's no way I can ever forgive Radek.

GAUZE

Dr Krzysztof Mazurkiewicz, emergency surgeon at Pomorskie Cent-
rum Traumatologii:

5:15 pm
The patient arrived in an extremely fragile state, with a hole in his
palate, and his gums riddled with bits of shell. Blood flow and swelling was obstructing his breathing, so I ordered an immediate endo-
tracheal intubation.

5:17 pm
One of the nurses called the police to report the hate crime.

5:19 pm
We tilted the head back into sniffing position to align the oral, pha-
ryngeal, and laryngeal axes. We pressed down on the patient's mandible to open the mouth as wide as possible. I inserted the laryngoscope
blade past the right side of the tongue and down the throat. A gust
of warm breath confirmed its position. Once the metal tip was in the
vallecula, I pulled the handle forward to reveal the epiglottis, and slid
the tube down to twenty-three centimetres, the standard insertion for
an adult male. There is blood everywhere.

5:20 pm
The patient breathed by ventilator while we prepared for the tracheostomy, continuing to clean his mouth. We removed the shrapnel by hand and the blood via suction vacuum. Because of the extensive blood loss, the patient was at severe risk for circulatory shock. We administered a clotting agent by injection, and the blood team took serum samples to find a type match, in case a transfusion became necessary.

5:22 pm
I took my gloves off temporarily, and held a finger against the patient's nose. Incidental breath is so beautiful, especially when you can barely feel it.

5:24 pm
We had just identified the Jackson's triangle and were about to perform the first tracheal incision when the patient's temperature and systolic pressure fell. The nurse called the police once again, and she spoke to the patient's friend in the waiting room (the one who had called for the ambulance), explaining that we couldn't perform the tracheostomy until his vital signs stabilized.

5:30 pm
Diastolic plummeted. The police still hadn't shown up to investigate, and I grew frustrated. I snapped at the nurses and told them to get lost, but they stuck around. So professional. Wish I could say the same for myself.

5:35 pm
Fuck this.

5:36 pm

It was against all training, all advice, all common sense to start the tracheostomy when the patient's vital signs were shit. It could throw his body into a tailspin and reduce his temperature to a chill. But something told me this kid needed to breathe, not through a ventilator, but through his fucking neck. Yes, I had to rip another hole into his body. Yes, I had to kick him when he was low and expose his insides to a roomful of bacteria. This was murder and this was saving him. I was confused, and I longed to feel more of his breath. The Hippocratic oath was supposed to distinguish killing from curing, but this was definitely a grey area.

5:38 pm

The nurse went to the waiting room again to give the patient's friend an update. The woman tried to fight her way into the OR, but security kept her out. Good thing, too. This was my boy. *My boy.* He looked exactly like Elvis. This tracheostomy meant so much more to me than the Pope's.

5:39 pm

No cops. Screw the cops, the homophobic bastards. I know what you're thinking: "I'm never going to the hospital again." Ha. Just wait. You will.

5:41 pm

The nurse brought me a can of orange Fanta. It helped.

Now pay close attention, because you'll probably have to perform this on yourself one day. I'm willing to bet money that someone out there wants you dead and that the bottom of their boot is the exact width of your throat. Treads matching wrinkles, even.

We made an incision between the suprasternal notch and the cricoid cartilage, then dissected the tissue with a cat's paw retractor. Once the tracheal rings were visible, we made another incision between the second and third rings, and injected a two percent silocaine solution into the windpipe to prevent cough.

5:47 pm

I inserted the tracheostomy tube, and held a piece of gauze in front of the nozzle to confirm its position.

This was the test.

The patient's breath would flutter the gauze with every inhale and exhale, strongly if he was going to make it. The systolic could lie, the diastolic could bluff, and the pulse could fluctuate wildly from minute to minute. But the patient's breath would animate the gauze, in movements that could not be denied.

That is, if we had gauze.

You see, I made this last part up, because I wanted so badly for it to be true. This was Gdańsk, not Rome. Hospital standards are shit in former Communist countries. In Gdańsk, they didn't think to check the OR's gauze supplies. We had none.

In Gdańsk, there were no steel bars to stop crazed women from trying to break in through the window while a surgery was in progress.

EKSTRA

Dear Magpie,

I have something to tell you. There are several people in my life who question your motives. They think you're trying to use me, and at first, I wondered if they were right. I've come to realize, however, that they're all assholes. I know you love me, because I can feel it. But even more than that, I think you and I were meant to be together.

How does one believe in destiny without believing in God? I apologize for being such a contradiction.

One more thing. In my first letter to you, I wrote about how the smell of smoke will never leave you. My description was accurate, but incomplete.

I hope you never have to feel the carbon molecule creep, the coughing, the tiny black mushrooms floating in your lungs, sucking your oxygen, raining acrid choking soot, dust, and the dry burn of ash in the nose, blackness with not a sunny patch of grey, everything spirited to smoke that has weight, buckets of fumes that crush you, eclipsing all light, pinching your nostrils and taping your face shut, parts of the world now living inside you, under your eyelids, in your rasping and charred throat, stealing more oxygen so you can't breathe in, burning plastic singeing, killing cells, turning you into a piece of smoke, coughing, choking, absorbing the physical world one element at a time, blinding tears that taste like wood, making memories, building sediment cakes inside you, making memories, can't exhale because more smoke will come in, flavouring your hair, making memories, staining you the colour of all things, raking heat through your chest, feels like gravel and baked blood, killing tissue, this horrible synthesis of elements forcing you to grow as a person, to change, the most wonderful thing there is ... how could you have missed it all this time?

Dear Magpie, smoke is the gift of memory. A fire at St Mary's would give us so much to remember. Think of the altarpiece burning for days, plumes and plumes of gold paint blackening the sky over all Kraków. It would be such a sight, or as you say, it would be "*ekstra*." How else could we possibly preserve all that we've been through? How would it live on?

Please reconsider the plan.

That's all for now. Sorry you got this letter so late. I didn't have a stamp.

Your Radeki

THE SMOK WAWELSKI

I had finally found a cave that suited me, but no matter which way I crawled in the darkness, the drops kept hitting me in the head. The worst part is that they smelled like gasoline. I'm a girl who doesn't need gas in her hair. Not even painful twists of the spine could manoeuvre me out of the way. Less flash-blind, and I would've been able to see.

I wasn't yet feeling right in my skin, in the bones of the new creature I knew I was becoming.

I did not leave Radek lying on a hospital gurney in Gdańsk. I had taken him with me—inside me—and he would live as long as my pH balance didn't snuff out the last of his embers.

But it was in that cave, the unlit concrete hollow beneath where the Dębnicki Bridge leaves land to span the Wisła River, where I first began to lose him. Feeling the crags in the nape of the steel anchorage, looking for the can of *barszcz* soup and the tin of *śledź* I'd picked up running away from the Stare Miasto and past the Sheraton Kraków, I couldn't even picture his face.

If I hadn't been so rushed, I could've found a better hiding place. At first, I ran away from the town square towards Wawel castle, certain I could find a derelict stone corner full of piss and anonymity. But there were too many tourists with cameras, so I ran toward the Wisła, guided by the fading glow in the sky.

Kraków became strange to me. This was not my city anymore, even though I'd just transformed part of it into a more inhabitable space. Then again, if I had ever been in love with Kraków, I wouldn't have touched a single brick.

I am writing this so you will understand why I did it.

My hiding place under the bridge wasn't as secure as I had originally thought. I could feel air sluicing through invisible holes in the ceiling, and I reached up to feel them. I slid my bony fingers up through the embrasures, the spaces between the interlocking metal teeth that reinforced sections of the asphalt deck. Such a small detail that you'd never notice it.

Radek never would have described my fingers as "bony," or noticed my calluses. His words? Surely "milky necks of baby swans" or something similar. What a psycho. I smiled and touched my swans, savouring the moment.

It had begun to rain. A car whooshed inches above my head, splashing water down onto me.

I was starving. I walked down to the river and smashed my can of *barszcz* against whatever sharp rocks I could find in the dark. It took a while, but I eventually made a few nicks and dents. When the can grew lighter, I read it as a sign of my growing strength, but I was really losing soup with every thrash, until almost nothing was left.

Rain started to dimple the water. I sat down on the gravel at the river's edge and peeled open my tin of *śledź*. The smell repulsed me. Herring should never be drowned in tomato sauce and lemon juice— I don't care *how* I preferred them in a past life. They should swim free and fresh and dead, their eye glaze clearly visible.

Like a good dragon, I washed the fish off in the river and had my first meal of the day.

I need to tell you about the embrasures.

Castles have embrasures. Wawel is full of them. They're the bevelled slats you shoot arrows through, wide on the inside and narrow on the exterior. You strike and your enemies can't strike back unless they have much better aim than you. It's a one-way assault.

When I noticed that my cave had these, I celebrated by writing my new name in gravel at the edge of my nook:

HOME OF THE SMOK WAWELSKI

It has always disturbed me that no one ever questioned the Smok's gender. Dragons can't all be guys. But I have bigger preoccupations. Why did Radek, the fire monomaniac and lifelong Kraków resident, never once talk about Kraków's Great Fire of 1850?

It hurts my brain just to think about it.

Go to the Dominican Church of the Holy Trinity, and sit wherever you like. You'll notice complete stillness. Even during the busiest mass, nothing moves. Look up. The nave is an almost endless indigo sky, with a skeleton of gilded piping. The lattice-work of God.

Now imagine a creeping roar filling the church from transept to transept and cavity to cavity, rotting the silence. The stained glass glows white and hot. Red cancels out green cancels out blue.

Saint Casimir melts.

Saint Ursula winks away a flame.

Saint Melchior Grodziecki dies again.

Saint Stanisław's forehead shatters.

The Five Holy Martyrs of Miedzyrzecz become one, as many worshippers already knew they were.

The church itself remains silent; all noise is the fire's.

Bricks crash from the ceiling until there are holes to heaven. You are immune to all this and stare right through the destruction. The lattice-work catches fire, brilliant licking yellow silhouetted against the black sky. The flaming ribcage of an animal on a spit. Then, a miracle happens. The church makes its first sound since it was built in the thirteenth century.

It sighs, knowing it has lost.

This fire of 1850 was *ekstra*. I can assure you that it was started by someone like me. Accidents don't happen that perfectly. There's always an architect behind them.

Ever since, bonfires have been prohibited in Kraków. You know, the kind of marshmallow parties that Radek staged at his gallery shows. It's as if he refused to honour the fire that had made his art illegal, even though it was probably the one he wished most to replicate. When you think about it, Kraków 1850 was the only fire that ever could've mattered to him.

But he never said a word about it, the bastard.

From my cave, I heard the watery shish of a car on the wet road approaching the bridge. Diesel, yes, but the engine didn't sound mercenary enough to be a bus or tank. I strained to listen, my ear pressed up to the embrasures, my body nearly upright but for a mild hunch. A few centimetres of me didn't fit. I saw the headlights waver as the car dipped on the uneven road.

It couldn't have been more than a hundred metres away when I heard the driver kill the engine. That is to say, the wheel splash got louder while the engine muffled to a choke (choked to a muffle? My English will never be as good as Radek's was).

Then there was no air, no light, and no sound. My nose filled with rust, the smell of the chassis. The car had rolled over my cave, sealing me in with a roof. I couldn't see the slick tires, but I could smell them.

Dragons, in case you didn't know, recognize rust as the smell of spilled blood oxidizing.

The passenger door opened, and then the driver's. Boots hit the pavement. I was ready with my knife—my tin can cover—and my specialized dragon weapon.

In my delirium, I made some last-minute hypotheses ... maybe it was just a few fishermen looking to skim easy kill from the surface of the Wisła. Rain brings out the gullible ones, whole schools of them ... or maybe it was Michał and that other boy from the Baltic, come to take me across the border to Prague for a few months ...

But no, these were nothing but literary fictions, tricks of the mind that the weak play on themselves. Play on their friends.

There's something I always wanted to tell Radek but never had the chance.

I used to believe we could change the world through literature, no matter what. We would till hearts slowly, a page at a time. But I've learned that books are useless in times of war: nobody has time to read them. What would I have done with Czesław Miłosz's *Piesek Przydrożny*, there under the bridge? Spit poetry at my pursuers? What bison shit.

I lit my blowtorch.

I heard the sound of footfalls on the gravel, coming from the side of the bridge. Flashlights played shakily down the embankment. Two cops came into view, guns drawn and pointed at me.

"Dorota Kubisz," the closest one said, "may God have mercy on you. Turn off the torch."

"He's dead," I said. "I am no longer afraid."

"Who's dead?"

"Radek."

"Did you kill someone, too? We have orders to shoot you."

"I didn't kill him," I said, showing my teeth. I opened the propane valve further and the blue flame turned orange and ragged. "You did."

"I could end your life with one bullet, you whore."

"But you won't do it. You want me in prison, so every priest in the fucking country can come to paint a picture of hell on the cell wall."

"I said turn it off."

"Tell me, how is the church of our mother?"

"You will never see it again."

"Because it's not there?"

He said nothing, and gave me a smug smile.

He must've known how painful his silence was to me. I was dying to know if the fire was still gutting St Mary's, or if my afternoon fire spree had been for nothing. Radek's last letter had eaten through my layers of niceness. I had to honour his final wish, or it would have continued chewing through my life until there was nothing left. Plus, I began to crave the smell of smoke. It was either the church or my own apartment.

But the officer wasn't going to tell me if St Mary's was now an ash heap. The second cop started speaking into his radio, walking in a wide circle across the mouth of my lair to the west side of the bridge, as if to block me from running.

"Where is the body of this Radek?" the smiling one asked.

But I wasn't listening. I lifted my weapon to the embrasures under the car. I could tell by the horror on their faces that they hadn't known about this construction detail on the bridge until I showed them. My interrogator screamed at his partner to move the car, but they were too late.

A dragon's blowtorch can get her into a lot of trouble.

Now, if Radek were here, he would explain how this little show had nothing to do with the gas tank and everything to do with the tires.

Burning tires, he would say, are the most difficult items on earth to extinguish. A single tire contains 7.5 litres of oil, and would smoulder for days.

You could extinguish the outside, but the inside would keep on burning.

You could put the fire out completely, but its own sustained heat would reignite the flame.

Tires are the most beautiful objects on earth, he would say.

DANIEL ALLEN COX is the author of *Shuck*, shortlisted for a Lambda Literary Award for debut fiction and the ReLit Award (Canada) for best novel. He is also a columnist for *Capital Xtra!* in Ottawa, Canada. He lives in Montreal; his home burned down in 2007.